"Please *God, help us*!"
Josh's screamed prayer came from
somewhere behind Mike.
He tried to concentrate on
getting control of the sub,
but depth charges kept going off
in his mind. Without warning
another series of real bombs exploded.

The adventure's not over when you're done reading the book!

Once you've read "Submarine Spy," ask Mom or Dad if you can visit our website. There you'll find:

- loads of other information about Mike, Josh, and the others
- Mike's sketches of the submarine
- a quiz to test your knowledge of the story
- Bible verses that go with the story
- maps of Seacrest and Admiralty Sound
- and much more!

www.JerichoQuill .com

Other books by Arnold Ytreeide

Check out our website for these and other titles:

The Jotham's Journey Trilogy – adventure books for the whole family to be read during the Christmas season or any other time:

- **Jotham's Journey**
- **Bartholomew's Passage**
- **Tabitha's Travels**

During Lent and the Easter season, or whenever you want another adventure:

- **Mystery of the Temple Court**

Just for fun!

- **Under My Teacher's Desk**

Visit our website for more books for **kids, teens, and adults!**

www.JerichoQuill.com

Mike Danford Adventure Series #1

Submarine Spy

Arnold Ytreeide

Jericho Quill Press

SUBMARINE SPY

ISBN: 978-1434833679

JQP 08-01

Printed in the United States of America

Jericho Quill Press
PO Box 252
Nampa, ID 83686

For Al Erickson -
who never shied away from
having an adventure
with me!

CHAPTER ONE
A STRANGE SIGHT

Mike Danford wiped the sweat from his forehead as the afternoon sun baked his broad shoulders. Icy saltwater washed across his bare feet. Flying chips of barnacle stung his skin as he continued hammering at the oily pilings.

Mike loved working at Seacrest Marina. Even now, when he had to chip barnacles off the elevator used to lift boats out of the water and up into the storage building above. It's the perfect way to earn extra money during spring vacation, he thought.

"Mike! Look out!" The sudden shout from high overhead stopped Mike in mid swing. "Runaway boat!" For a second he hesitated, wondering if this was a joke. Standing on the elevator he couldn't see the boat inside the building above. But then he heard the wheels of the boat dolly thundering like a freight train and knew he only had seconds to act.

Mike saw the bow of the runaway boat break through the safety gate fifty feet over his head, sending splintered wood in every direction. He spun around to the open side of the platform and dove headfirst into the icy waters of Admiralty Sound, praying the boat would miss him. As he plunged deep below the surface, the cold water stabbed at Mike's skin like needles. His eyes stung from the salt in the water, but he forced himself to keep them open. Pushing against the green water, his powerful arms and legs stroked and kicked. But he had moved only a few feet before he heard, and then felt, the thirty foot cabin cruiser crash through the floor of the elevator he had been standing on moments before. The impact created a great wave of seawater that picked Mike up and tossed him through the air like a piece of driftwood. When he splashed down again he was looking up at the bottom of the boat.

The cruiser paused, standing straight up for a split second, then began falling directly toward Mike. His heart pounding, he kicked wildly, but could only watch as the towering vessel fell, its twin brass propellers threatening to slice him to pieces.

For an instant, Mike saw something strange on the bottom of the boat. He didn't know what it was, but it didn't look like anything he had ever seen. Seconds later the white fiberglass hull smashed into the water only inches from his head.

The force of the impact sent Mike flying on a second wall of water. He tried to swim to safety but the power of the wave grabbed him like the hand of a giant and flung him toward the gas dock. In the next moment everything went black as he slammed headfirst into a piling.

"Mike! Can you hear me?" The voice seemed to echo from the far end of a tunnel as Mike struggled to wake up. Slowly, he began opening his eyes, blinking rapidly as the harsh sunlight flooded in. Finally he realized he was lying on the cold, wet wood of the marina gas dock. A blanket covered his shivering body as several people huddled around. One of the faces staring down at him was saying something.

"Mike. It's Josh. Are you okay?"

As the fog cleared, Mike looked at the frightened face through blurry eyes. He finally recognized it to be his best friend, Josh Roberts.

"Josh?" he said slowly, "What are you doing here?"

Josh broke into a wide grin at the sound of his friend's voice. "Oh, I had nothing better to do so I thought I'd come down and watch you sleeping on the job."

Mike raised up on his elbows and looked at the crowd that had gathered. He mentally checked each part of his body and decided that, except for the awful pain at the back of his head, he was more-or-less okay. "Very funny, Joshua. Why don't you be useful and help me up."

Before Josh could reply, another voice interrupted. "Whoa there, young fella, you just stay put."

The voice was that of Captain Washington from the fire department, who was pushing through the crowd. "We'll just have a look at you before you go running off." Just then an aid car, its lights flashing, pulled up behind the captain's car.

Even without his booming voice, Captain Washington would be a hard man to refuse. His six-foot frame, big muscles, and firm jaw left little doubt who was in charge.

"Honest, Cap, I'm really okay," Mike pleaded.

The dark brown skin of the captain's forehead wrinkled into a concerned frown. "How about you let us be the judge of that?"

Mike resigned himself to his fate as the Emergency Medical Technicians started poking and prodding his body. The crowd began moving off, and Josh sat on the railing of the dock, enjoying his friend's predicament.

"Your name, please," a young firefighter asked, filling out a form.

"Mike Danford...er...Michael James Danford."

"Age?"

"Seventeen."

"Height and weight?"

"Five foot eleven, a hundred-sixty pounds."

"Hair color is light brown . . . what color are your eyes?" the firefighter asked.

"Why do you need to know . . . oh, never mind. They're green."

The questions and exam seemed endless. Finally, Captain Washington stood, removing a stethoscope from his ears. "Well, there are no broken bones and it doesn't look like you have a concussion. You do have a nasty bump on the head, though. I'd suggest you have a doctor take a look at it."

"Thanks Cap, I'll do that."

The Captain turned to Josh. "You'd best get your friend here home and into some dry clothes."

"Sure thing, Cap," Josh replied. He jumped down from the railing and extended a long, muscular arm to Mike. "Come on, water boy, time to get you beached."

It was only then that Mike noticed that Josh's clothes were also dripping. "How come *you're* all wet?" he asked his friend.

Josh gave him a grin and said, "How do you think you got out of the water?"

Mike looked at his friend and rescuer and said, "Thanks Josh. I owe you one."

"I know," Josh grinned back.

With Josh's help, Mike stood up, holding onto the railing to steady himself. Then he reached in his pocket and pulled out a couple of soggy watermelon-flavored Jolly Ranchers. "Want one?" he asked Josh seriously. Josh gave him a sick look. "There's nothing wrong with these," Mike said. To prove his point, he unwrapped one and popped it in his mouth. "Just a little salty," he reported. Josh just shook his head in disgust.

As they climbed the ramp from the dock up to the parking lot, Mike and Josh looked over at the scene of the accident. A crew of men were moving a crane into position on the dock to raise the boat that had almost crushed Mike. The sight of the smashed elevator sent a chill up Mike's spine. I could have been killed, he thought with a shiver.

"How'd it happen, anyway?" Josh asked.

"I don't know," Mike answered, slurping around the Jolly Rancher. "I was working down on the elevator and just heard someone yell something about a runaway boat." He paused for a moment, sucking on the candy, staring at the scene below. Then he forced himself to stop shivering and decided to lighten the mood. He grinned at Josh and said, "The next thing I knew I was looking into your ugly face!"

"Very funny. You must still be delirious."

Josh was slightly taller and bigger than Mike, with darker brown hair. The two had been best friends since the second grade.

The police arrived and talked to Mike for a few minutes, then the boys climbed into Josh's red '67 Mustang and drove the three blocks up the hill to the Danford house. After hot showers and changes of clothes -- Josh always seemed to have at least half his clothes at Mike's house -- Mike got a couple cans of pop and joined his friend in the family room. The rest of the afternoon was spent telling and re-telling the story to Mike's parents, his two sisters, and the many friends that stopped by.

The only other interruption in the afternoon was a quick trip to the doctor. "Really, Mom, I'm okay," Mike had pleaded.

"That's for the doctor to decide," was her firm answer. "If I can have my appendix removed by a cook in a little shack on top of a mountain in Nepal, you can have a bump on the head looked at by a doctor in Seacrest."

Mike sighed and resigned himself to his fate, but made Josh go along with him.

"Did that really happen to your mom?" Josh whispered to his friend, always amazed at her stories.

Mike nodded. "One of the other climbers did the surgery while a doctor told him what to do over the radio." Mike's mother was a freelance writer who sold articles to magazines around the world. Before settling down to raise her family, she had traveled all over, met dozens of interesting people, and been on many hair-raising adventures.

"No concussion, and no serious injury," the doctor reported an hour later. Mike smiled and let out a relieved sigh.

"Can't you operate, just to be sure?" Josh said from across the chrome-and-white treatment room.

"Afraid not," the doctor laughed. "But if it'll make you feel better, I'm giving Mike a tetanus shot, just in case."

Josh grinned and Mike moaned, but took the shot without complaint.

That night the boat accident was at the top of the news and on the front page of the paper and internet sites. The small town of Seacrest wasn't big enough to have its own newspaper or television, but reporters from the nearby big cities had flocked to the scene. By the time they got there, though, the boat was gone and Mike had already left.

"Oh no!" Mike groaned as the TV news showed a picture of him from the previous year's school annual. "I look like I just woke up!" Although Mike was obviously younger in the picture, he had the same straight hair pushed back across his eyes, and the same tanned skin. The photographer had snapped the picture at just the wrong second, though, and Mike's eyes were half closed.

"Don't worry," Josh laughed, "everyone will just think you were hit by the boat and feel sorry for you."

Later, the Danfords and Josh had just sat down to dinner when there was a knock at the door. Mike answered it.

"Mike! Are you all right?"

It was his boss, Jordan Washington, Captain Washington's son, and owner of the marina. Though he was as tall as his father, Jordan had a much thinner build.

"Sure, Jordan. It's just a little bump on the head." Mike waved for his boss to come in.

"I was up in Conroy all day meeting with some people. Dad called me on my cell phone and told me about the accident. I can't believe this could happen!"

"Well, I'm okay, but the boat probably isn't," Mike said.

"No, it's not," Jordan answered, relaxing a little now that he saw Mike was fine. "I talked to Jake before coming over here and he said it was totaled." Jake Burton was another worker at the marina. "It's the owner's own fault, though. The boat belongs to that weird guy, Elmer Baker."

"Isn't that the guy who won't let anyone near his boat?" Josh asked.

"That's right," Jordan replied. "That's what caused the accident. He was trying to move the boat out of its compartment by himself and lost control of it."

The marina stored boats on three floors. Each boat had its own space, but some people paid extra for a compartment they could lock. When a boat owner wanted to go for a cruise, their boat would be taken out of its space, moved over to the elevator platform at the end of the building, and lowered into the water.

Mr. Danford, a wise-looking man in his early forties, spoke up. "Why won't this man let anyone near his boat, Jordan?"

"No one knows, Ben. He keeps it locked up and moves it himself on a special dolly. That is, he did before tonight. From now on we have a new policy at Seacrest Marina: only employees move boats!"

"Good decision," Mr. Danford said, looking at Mike.

"You'd think the man would at least come over and apologize for almost killing our son!" Mrs. Danford said. "Well anyway, it's over now. We'd better have dinner before it gets cold. You'll join us, won't you, Jordan?"

"Oh, no thanks Laura, I've got to get down to the marina and survey the damage." With that, Jordan said his goodbyes and left.

The boat accident was all they talked about during dinner. Mike's head still hurt but he was feeling much better. Afterward, Mike couldn't stand being locked up in the house anymore, so he and Josh took a walk in the warm spring air. Eventually they ended up at Seacrest's waterfront.

The town of Seacrest sat at the edge of Admiralty Sound. Protected from the ocean by a peninsula, Admiralty Sound was usually calm. Seacrest itself was also very quiet, except for the summer tourist season when people would flock there to boat, fish, sail, scuba dive and sun themselves on the beach. Small shops and restaurants lined the main road along the water. The rest of the town was made up of tree-lined streets and attractive homes on the steep hillside overlooking the Sound.

Mike and Josh walked to the marina and sat on the pier railing. Looking down toward the water they saw workmen repairing the damaged elevator under powerful floodlights. A cool breeze carried the smells of Admiralty Sound across the dock. Sucking on a strawberry-flavored Jolly Rancher, Mike took a deep breath and said, "I love the smell of salt water!"

Josh turned to him with a grin. "I know," he said. "You tell me that every time we come down here."

Mike pretended to be mad and knocked Josh off the railing. The two were having a friendly wrestling match when Jake Burton, a crusty old sea veteran, walked up and interrupted. After asking about Mike's health, the conversation turned to the salvage of the boat.

"It were just plain loony," Jake drawled. A lifetime resident of Seacrest, Jake's wind-worn face had seen sixty years of boats enter and leave the tiny cove. Running a crooked hand through his pure white crewcut, Jake looked perplexed.

"You hadn't even been yanked out'o the water before that Elmer Baker feller was on his cell phone callin' fer a crane. Twern't twenty minutes before the monster got here and Baker had his own divers going after the boat. Then he made us all leave before his crew brought the thing up. I tell ya it's just plain spooky."

"I wonder what he's trying to hide," Josh said. When Mike didn't answer, Josh looked over and saw him staring into space. "Uh oh, I've seen that look before."

Still lost in thought, Mike ignored his friend. "Jake, after the police interviewed everyone else, did they talk to Baker?"

"Well now, that's another strange thing," Jake replied. "Soon as ole Baker caught sight of them police cars he high-tailed it outta there. I never did see if the police cornered him. Didn't much matter, though. Everyone said it were just an ac-see-dent."

Mike suddenly jumped down from the railing. "Well, thanks Jake. I guess we'll high-tail it outta here ourselves," he said quickly. Grabbing Josh firmly by the arm and ignoring his objections, Mike dragged Josh off the pier toward the street.

"Uh, see you later Jake," Josh yelled over his shoulder. Then softly to Mike, "What's the matter with you? Did that blow on the head soften your brain?"

Away from the other people now, Mike stopped and looked at Josh. "Just the opposite, my brain finally started working! I didn't remember it until just now when Jake was talking about the boat . . . ."

"Remember what? What are you talking about?"

"Something I saw just before I was knocked out."

Mike tried to continue but his words were drowned out by the high-pitched scream of a revved-up engine. Both boys looked up the street in the direction of the noise. Headed straight at them at full throttle was a sleek black motorcycle!

CHAPTER TWO
A PLAN REVEALED

Mike froze in shock. The bike was coming fast, accelerating, and was aimed straight at him. His legs felt trapped in cement as he tried to move. An instant before the cycle would have rammed them, the boys dove out of its path.

Stunned but unhurt, Mike watched as the driver slid the bike into a tight turn. Blue smoke poured out from behind it, and the cycle once again came shrieking toward him. As it flashed under a street light, Mike saw that the driver was dressed all in black, with a black helmet and tinted face shield.

Reacting more quickly now, Mike and Josh sprang to their feet and ran in opposite directions. The biker followed Mike as he ducked into a nearby alley. Mike dove behind a garbage dumpster and was almost hit as the bike went by.

Refusing to give up, the madman spun his bike around for a fresh attack. Mike didn't trust the dumpster to protect him a second time and headed back to the street. Breathing hard, feet pounding, he realized too late that he would never beat the motorcycle to the alley entrance.

Mike forced his legs to pump faster but he looked back and saw the headlight just a few yards behind him. In that moment another movement caught his eye and he saw Josh throw a large piece of driftwood at the motorcycle's wheels. The driftwood caught the spokes and the bike went crashing to the ground.

Sparks flew everywhere as the twisted metal screeched across the pavement and crashed into the seawall overlooking the water. The driver was thrown clear, then jumped up and ran back toward his bike. Before he could reach it, Josh brought him down with a flying tackle. The smaller frame of the driver couldn't overcome Josh's body-builder strength, though, and he quickly lost the fight.

Mike ran up to help, but just then the driver wrenched his hand free and caught Josh with a surprise right hook to the jaw. Josh reeled backwards, dazed by the blow. The attacker quickly jumped up, ran to the bike and with one kick had it running again. Mike reached the spot just in time to grab wildly at the assailant's leather coat. He missed, and the bike sped down the street, turning up the hill away from the water.

From the opposite end of town a siren wailed, but Mike knew the police would never be able to catch the biker.

"Oh, my jaw!" Josh sat up slowly, holding his chin in his hands. "That guy must have had a brick in his hand."

"That guy must have had a brick in his *head*!" Mike answered. "Why would anyone want to run us down?"

Josh was getting to his feet. "Yeah, nice loveable guys like us."

The police car rolled up and Mike gave the officer a description of the bike, which he quickly relayed to the other patrol cars. Mike and Josh told the officer exactly what had happened, ending with the fact that there had been no license plate or other identifying marks on the bike. Mike's parents arrived and the boys went through the story again.

"So you have no idea who might have wanted to do this?" the officer asked.

"None at all," Mike said. "As far as I know I haven't made anyone *that* mad at me."

"Danford . . . aren't you the kid that almost got crushed by that boat today?"

"Uh, yes sir, that's me."

"You've had quite a day." Then turning to Mike's parents, "I'll stop by tomorrow and let you know what we dig up on this biker."

After the police officer left, the Danfords and Josh began the short walk home. The cool night air still carried the scent of salt water and the walk helped Mike calm down a little.

"That's twice today that God has protected you," Mr. Danford said.

"Yeah," Mike said, "and I'll be thanking Him for it tonight!"

After a few moments of silence Josh said, "I don't get it. Why would someone try to run us over?"

"It's a fact of life that some people do things just to be mean," Mr. Danford said.

"Maybe so," Josh replied, "but things like this aren't supposed to happen in Seacrest!"

The next morning came and went as Mike's body slept off the abuse of the day before. Finally, the sound of his bedroom door slamming shut brought him back to life. Through sleepy eyes he watched Josh enter the room and drape himself across an overstuffed chair in the corner.

"Time to get up, water boy."

Mike groaned, rubbing the lump on the back of his head. "What time is it?"

"Well, let's just say they're no longer serving lunch at Salty's Diner."

Mike sat up in shock. "Oh no! I'm late for work -- Jordan'll kill me. I was supposed to clean the Garcia boat today!"

"Relax. Jordan called your mom this morning and insisted you take the day off. *With* pay. Besides, you're not going anywhere until you finish telling me what you saw on that boat yesterday."

Mike had forgotten all about his interrupted story of the night before. He climbed out of bed and pulled on some jeans as he slowly began relating the incident.

"You have to understand that I'm not at all sure of what I saw. It all happened so fast . . . it's kind of a blur. Maybe it's nothing. It just seems sort of strange."

"All right already, I promise not to laugh. What is it?"

Mike moved over to the chair at his neatly organized desk, which was a contrast to his messy room. Taking a deep breath, he blurted out his suspicions. "I think Elmer Baker is a smuggler!"

Josh's mouth dropped open in surprise. "The owner of the runaway boat?" After several seconds he leaned forward, his chin resting in his hands. "Okay, you've got my attention. What makes you think Baker's a smuggler?"

Mike absent-mindedly played with the keys of his computer, trying to recall exactly what he had seen. "After the boat hit the water, it was standing straight up in the air. As it came toward me I saw a square hatch on the bottom. Just in front of that there was a thing sticking out that looked like a Christmas tree. It had several circular metal plates on a rod, and the circles got smaller as they got farther away from the boat."

Josh stared at Mike, and Mike stared back. "That's it?" Josh asked finally. "A door and a Christmas tree?"

"You said you wouldn't laugh."

"I'm *not* laughing. I just don't see what's so suspicious about it, that's all."

"There isn't anything like it on any other boat in the marina! What could it be used for?"

"What do *you* think it could be used for?"

Frustrated by his friend's lack of insight, Mike grasped for possibilities. "I don't know, maybe the Christmas tree is a way of snagging bags of drugs. Maybe divers use the door to deliver guns. Maybe it's a way of homing in on a stash . . ."

"Or maybe," Josh injected quietly, "it's just a fancy depth finder for a guy who likes to go fishing a lot." He leaned back in the chair. "Anyway, we'll never know because they hauled the boat off yesterday and no one's seen ole Elmer ever since."

"I guess you're right, it was probably nothing," Mike conceded. "It just bugs me when I can't figure something out."

Josh laughed. "Don't I know it!" Mike grinned back, remembering some of the episodes they had been through. When they were ten, Mike took apart Josh's CD player so they could use the laser inside to cut holes in pop cans. It never worked. When they were twelve, he got them both in trouble when he tried to motorize their skateboards. And just two years before he had knocked out all the power in the neighborhood when he tried to make Josh's TV work in 3-D.

"So I'm the curious type, " Mike said. "At least we haven't been bored!" They laughed again, then Mike said, "But I still want to know what was on the bottom of that boat. It bothers me."

Josh stood and crossed to the desk. "Well, I know something that will take your mind off it. Have you forgotten what today is?"

Mike snapped up straight. "The plans!"

"That's right, the plans. Today we unveil your brilliant design skills to your parents, and try to convince them to let you spend your life savings on a hunk of metal."

"It's *not* a hunk of metal," Mike protested, punching his friend in the gut. "It's a highly technical piece of machinery."

"To you and me it's a highly technical piece of machinery. To your parents it'll be a several-thousand-dollar hunk of metal."

"Maybe, but I'll give it my best shot. Right after dinner tonight. You gonna be here?"

"Wouldn't miss it. It's been a long time since I've seen you cry."

As they laughed together, Mike thought back to a time when Josh had been the one crying. Shortly after he'd turned eight, Josh's father had been killed in an accident. Since then his mother had to work a lot to pay the bills, so Josh had become almost like a brother to Mike. In fact he had even told Mike once that he kind of thought of Mike's dad as his own, which didn't bother Mike one bit.

The boys spent the rest of the day lying on Seacrest Beach. There were only two days left of spring break, and everyone was taking full advantage of the nice weather. Though Seacrest itself only had a population of five thousand, sunny days always brought people flocking to the waterfront from all over. Several of Mike's friends from school were there, and no one knew who the mysterious biker could be.

"You haven't got an enemy in the whole school," one girl said.

"Someone sure had it in for us," Mike answered, the Jolly Rancher in his mouth making it sound slurred. "Josh has the sore jaw to prove it."

Just then another voice interrupted. "That's nothing compared to the time I fought off a motorcycle gang." The new speaker was Nick Travis, who had just walked up to the group. "They had knives and chains, and all I had were my bare hands."

The whole group moaned in disgust.

"Come on, Travis, give it up," one boy said. "We don't believe you for a second."

Nick was one of the least popular guys in the school, mainly because he was always bragging and lying. Mike was the only one who even tried to be his friend.

"Why don't you just be yourself, Nick?" Mike said. "You don't need to make up stories."

"I *did* fight a bike gang," Nick yelled, "and if you don't believe me it's your problem, not mine." With that he kicked sand in their direction and stomped off.

"Poor Nick," Mike sighed. "He'd be okay if he'd just quit lying."

Josh was not so generous. "Why do you even pay attention to him, Mike? He's a jerk!"

"Maybe if more people paid attention to him, he wouldn't be such a jerk," Mike said. Then he sighed and added, "It just seems like the right thing to do." Josh just stared at the sand in silence.

The rest of the day passed and soon it was time for dinner. Josh, the eternal dinner guest, helped Mike's mother set the table while Mike helped his older sister with her homework.

"It's easy, sis. Just multiply the figures in the brackets, divide by four, and add that to the sum of the first equation."

Amy Danford gave her brother an exasperated look. "Why do I need to know algebra anyway? I'm an *art* major!"

"Don't try to explain it to him," Josh yelled from the kitchen. "He thinks the whole world revolves around math!"

"It *does!*" Mike yelled back.

Conversation during dinner drifted from the boat accident, to the motorcycle attack, to the latest sale at the mall. Mrs. Danford reported that the police had been by, but had no information on the mysterious motorcycle attack. "Your sister called this afternoon, too," she said.

"Katie?" Mike brightened. "What did she want?"

"To see how you were feeling," Laura Danford said. "Your accident was even in her college newspaper." Then she added, "I just told her you were too busy talking to all the girls on the beach to come to the phone."

Mike blushed. "I think I could have torn myself away to talk to my sister."

It was Amy's turn to do the dishes, so after dinner Mike nervously asked his parents if he and Josh could talk to them in the den. They gathered around his father's polished wood desk. Mike felt like he was in the principal's office as he began.

"You know I've been saving my money from the marina to buy a car and for college. Well, I've decided there's something else I'd like to spend it on, if it's okay with you." He hesitated, searching for the right words.

"Yes Mike, what is it?" Ben Danford tried to calm his son's nerves. "We're listening."

"Well," Mike continued, "it's kind of . . . uh . . . no, it's more like . . . well you see, I always wanted . . ." Finally in frustration he grabbed a large set of drawings and rolled them out onto the desk in one swift motion. "It's a submarine!"

Mike's parents gasped at the plans before them. "Mike, did *you* draw these?" Mr. Danford asked.

"Yes sir. On my computer. I used the plotter at school to print them out. I have all the calculations here, and I know it will work, if you'll just give me time to show you . . . ."

Mike knew he'd have no trouble getting his parents to listen. Getting them to agree might be a different matter.

For the next two hours Mike went over every detail of the plan. The drawings showed a small submarine with enough room for four people to sit, one behind another. The sub looked like a large steel pipe with a plexiglass bubble on the front, and a cone-shaped projection in the back which housed two electric motors. Small wing-like diving planes and a rudder would make the sub go up and down and turn. A conning tower on top held the hatch, periscope, antennas, and an emergency marker buoy that could be released if the sub got into trouble.

Two pipes, as big around as car tires, ran along the bottom of the sub and had round caps at each end. Water could be pumped in and out of these "pontoons" to make the sub rise or sink. Mike, with Josh's help, had carefully planned every detail of the submarine, and the drawings showed exactly how it would be built. A ream of computer printouts contained every calculation and stress projection.

When at last Mike had finished explaining the features of the sub, Mr. Danford sat back with his hands clasped behind his head. "I'm very impressed, Mike! You've done an outstanding job of designing this submarine. I take it you want to build this yourself?"

"That's right, Dad. Josh and I already talked to Mr. Johnson, the shop teacher, and he said we can use the school's shop. He also promised to help us in any way possible."

"What about materials? Is everything you need available? And more importantly, can you afford it?"

"We made a complete list of parts," Mike pulled out another printout, "and estimated what each would cost. A lot of it we'd get at the Aerospace Surplus Store. The hull and Plexiglass would have to be specially made and would be the most expensive."

Mike's mother gasped and his father gave a low whistle as they saw the total price. "That's just about everything you have saved, Mike," his mother said. Then his father added, "That's a lot of money for a . . ." he almost called it a toy but thought better of it, ". . . for something that won't even take you to the grocery store."

Mike thought desperately, trying to convince his father. "It could take me to the store on Fox Island," he offered weakly.

Mr. Danford smiled. "I know you really want this, son, but it just doesn't seem very . . . practical."

"It's not *supposed* to be practical," he pleaded. "It's supposed to be fun and adventurous! It's supposed to be for exploring places no one has ever been before, right here in Admiralty Sound. It's supposed to be for studying marine life." Mike jumped to his feet and began pacing the floor as he spoke. "It's for teaching me and anyone else that wants to come along about life under the water . . . for helping people find things they've lost . . . inspecting piers and bulkheads."

Mike's mind was racing as he tried to put into words all the things he was feeling. "It's for satisfying my own curiosity about life!" He paused and dropped his voice a notch. "I guess most of all it's to prove to myself that I can do it, that my plans would really work."

When Mike had finished his plea, Mr. Danford sat back, thinking for a few moments. "So this is what you two have been up to all this time," he said with a smile.

"Yes sir," Mike answered.

After another moment of consideration, Mr. Danford said, "Son, why don't you and Josh leave us alone for a few minutes so we can talk it over."

"Sure, Dad." Both boys left, quietly closing the door behind them.

"What do you think?" Josh asked his friend.

Mike was glum. "I think the only way I'm going to get underwater is with a mask and snorkel."

Both boys sat waiting on the front steps of the house. Mike offered Josh a Jolly Rancher, which he accepted. "You know your mother's right," Josh said. "The way you eat these, some day your teeth really *will* fall out."

Mike shook his head. "No way," he said with a slurp. "They're sugarless!"

The few minutes his father had asked for turned into half an hour, then an hour. Finally, the door opened and Mr. Danford called them in.

"First, Mike, let me say again how impressed I am with your plans. I know you've spent months of hard work on this and I'm proud of you . . ."

Mike's heart fell as he waited for the 'but' that he could tell was coming.

"But," Mr. Danford continued, "I also know how dangerous this can be. Even one small mistake could bring tragic results."

Mike was no longer listening. It was obvious what was coming and all he could think of was the hundreds of hours of wasted work.

"That's why I've spent the last forty-five minutes on the phone with a friend of mine, Admiral Norton over at the Keyport Submarine Base . . ."

Why couldn't his father understand? Mike knew he had to be careful, but with proper testing they could make sure the sub was safe.

"And he agreed with me that it could be extremely dangerous. Designing a submarine takes a great deal of engineering and mathematics, and years of special training."

Mike had known all along that his parents would probably say no, but now that it was really happening he just couldn't believe it.

"So I made arrangements for you to take the plans over to him, and if he says they're okay, you can build your submarine."

"But *Dad*, you don't understand . . . ." Mike stopped as he realized his mother, father and Josh were grinning at him. "What did you say?"

"I said if Admiral Norton okays your plans, you can build the sub. He's been designing submarines since World War II and he'll know if your plans are safe."

Mike jumped up with a yell. "That's great, Dad. I know he'll approve them."

Josh thumped his friend on the back. "Congratulations, water boy."

"There are a few other conditions," Mr. Danford said. "I want every weld x-rayed for flaws, and I'll personally supervise a complete testing program. *And*," he added, "it must be licensed by the American Bureau of Submarines. But from what I've seen here, I don't think you'll have any problems. Remember, though, Admiral Norton's decision is final."

"I'll get those plans over to him right away. Thanks Dad, thanks Mom. I promise I'll build it safe."

"Well, just make sure you leave plenty of time to take me on rides," his mother said. "I want to see what's down there. There's got to be a magazine article in this somewhere!"

Josh stayed with Mike that night and they talked about the project until just before dawn, when they finally fell asleep exhausted. Mike was awake by nine, though, and kicked Josh to wake him up.

"What are you doing awake in the middle of the night?" Josh mumbled.

"It's almost nine," Mike said. "It's immoral to sleep any later than this."

"You thought it was moral yesterday."

"Yesterday I didn't have to go see Admiral Norton."

"Okay, okay, I'm up." Josh's head emerged from the end of the sleeping bag he was in.   Mike was already up and pulling on his clothes. "I'll go call the Admiral while you take a shower."

"Good plan," Josh mumbled.

"Be right back." Mike closed the door as he left, and Josh promptly pulled the sleeping bag back over his head.

Two hours later the two friends were on their way to the Navy base. Keyport was the center for all nuclear subs in the Pacific Ocean, and was located on a peninsula directly west of Seacrest. It was about a two-hour drive around the shores of Admiralty Sound, and the boys spent the time talking about the hundreds of things to be done. The convertible top of Josh's Mustang was down, letting the wind and sun slap them in the face.

As they reached the peninsula and turned north, Josh changed the subject. "I don't mean to sound paranoid, but I think someone's following us."

Mike turned at once and looked out the back. "There are at least twenty cars back there, how can you tell?"

"I've been watching him in the rear view mirror. It's the dark green four-door about six cars back. He's made every turn we have since we left Seacrest."

"Maybe he's just going the same direction we are?"

Josh glanced at his friend. "What are the chances of someone else from Seacrest going to Keyport at the same time we are?"

"Pretty low," Mike agreed.

"Exactly. Anyhow, I'm going to find out for sure. Hold on."

At the next intersection, Josh waited until the last possible second then swerved the car sharply to the right, turning down a side road. He punched the accelerator, the force pushing them back in their seats. Mike looked back and saw the green sedan drifting around the corner, tires smoking. "Looks like you were right, they're on our tail!"

The two-lane road wound around through the grassy hills of the peninsula and Josh took the curves as fast as he safely could. As they crested a hill there was another intersection ahead and Josh made a fast left turn. Running quickly through the gears, he wound out the speedometer in just a few seconds. He wasn't quick enough, though, and their tail came over the hill in time to see Josh's car headed down the side road. Only then did Mike see the sign that read DEAD END.

CHAPTER THREE
A SICKENING SURPRISE

"Now what?" Josh yelled as he crammed the car into fourth gear.

"Maybe we can find someplace to hide down here," Mike answered.

"We'd better. I don't think these guys are from the Prize Patrol!"

Josh pulled out a cell phone and tossed it to Mike. "You'd better call the police!"

Mike looked at the screen and groaned. "No Service," he read, which meant they were too far from a cellular tower for the signal to reach.

"Maybe we should pray," Mike said.

"Couldn't hurt," Josh replied.

As Josh maneuvered the car, Mike said a quick prayer. "Lord, please help us!"

"Yes Lord, please help us," Josh echoed.

A few seconds later the boys rounded a curve. Mike gasped and his mouth fell open. Parked on the side of the road was a county sheriff's car with a deputy standing next to it.

The officer gaped as the boys sped by, locked up the brakes and spun around. As they pulled in behind the police car, the green sedan came around the corner. The driver instantly saw the police officer and put the sedan into a four-wheel skid. Before anyone had time to react, the other car had burned a one-eighty in the middle of the road and headed back the way it had come.

Mike and Josh ran up to the deputy yelling for him to chase the car, but he couldn't understand what they were saying. "Hold on there, gentlemen. One at a time." He turned to Mike. "What's going on here?"

Mike tried to slow himself down, and explained the situation to the officer. The deputy then got on the radio and gave the information to the dispatcher.

"Why don't you go after them?" Mike pleaded.

"Well now I'd love to, but these cars don't run so good on three wheels."

Mike and Josh looked as the officer pointed to his right rear tire, which was flat. "You're lucky someone forgot to put a spare in this car, or I would have been gone by now. In fact, you're lucky I was here at all. I've patrolled this part of the county for six months and this is the first time I've ever been down this road."

The two boys looked at each other in amazement. "I don't think it was luck," Mike said softly.

They finished signing the police report just as a county maintenance truck arrived to fix the tire. They thanked the officer and went back to their car. Once there, they sat in silence for a moment.

"It really works," Mike said quietly.

"What works?" Josh asked.

"Prayer."

Josh nodded silently, then said, "I guess so."

The rest of the trip to Keyport went smoothly with no sign of the green sedan. They identified themselves to the guards at the gate, then found their way to Admiral Norton's wood-paneled office in a cinder-block building.

The admiral looked impressive in his blue uniform with gold stripes on each sleeve. He's only as tall as I am, Mike thought, but he seems a foot taller!

The admiral greeted the boys warmly, and introduced them to his aide, Commander Ramsey. Mike noted that the commander wore a blue work uniform, and that the small silver oak leaf on his collar wasn't nearly as impressive as the admiral's stripes and star.

Admiral Norton had Commander Ramsey get them each a Coke, then began poring over the plans. "What do you estimate your maximum depth will be?" the admiral asked Mike as he began.

"It's right here on the computer printout . . . uh, around three hundred feet."

For more than three hours the admiral checked and re-checked the figures and specifications of Mike's plans. Mike squirmed in his red leather chair, nervously waiting for the admiral's verdict. He'll never go for it, he thought to himself. He looked at Josh, who just shrugged.

"I see you've included hover tanks," the admiral said. "What about a Q tank?" On and on it went, the admiral questioning Mike on every detail of the plan. "Have you calculated the sea slap forces on your front viewport?" he asked. Mike pointed to a set of figures. A few minutes later the admiral said, "You've included twin contra-rotating propellers, but have you considered using ducted propulsors?"

Finally, Admiral Norton sat back, frowned, and pointed to one of the equations on the printout. "I take it this is your calculated stress concentration factor?"

"Yes sir," Mike said with a gulp.

"Well, I'm afraid you made a mistake here. You've estimated the sub could dive to three hundred feet, but you based that figure on this incorrect data. The stress factor should really be . . ."

The admiral's fingers raced over the keyboard of his desk-side computer. Mike felt the sweat trickle down his neck as he watched, hoping the sub would be able to reach at least *two* hundred feet. He held his breath as the admiral finished.

"There we are. If my computations are correct, and I'll check them again, your sub should easily be able to dive to fifteen hundred feet."

Mike stared in disbelief.

"Fifteen . . . hundred?" he whispered.

"Feet?" Josh added.

"That's right. Mike, you've done an incredible job. You've designed a sub that will carry four people to depths few men have ever seen. Your design may not be pure genius, but it's very, very good. I fully approve of the plans and I'll tell your father that when I talk to him."

Mike could barely keep from shouting his excitement. "Uh, if it's not too much trouble," he said with a grin, "could you call him right now?"

The admiral looked at Mike and laughed. "Sure, why not." He placed the call, and it was obvious that Mike's father was also surprised at the estimated maximum depth. "Not that I'd take her down that deep on the first manned dive," Admiral Norton said into the phone, "but it should be capable of it."

After the Navy man got off the phone, he gave some pointers to Mike on building the sub. "And if you need more help, just go to this URL," he wrote down an internet address, "and you can tie in to my design programs." He gave Mike the secret address to his internet site, along with a low-level password.

The admiral then treated the boys to dinner at the Officer's Club where they talked more about the project. "I'd better be invited to the first cruise," he warned in mock seriousness.

"You can count on it," Mike replied.

"Also, I'd like you two to come over some time when you can stay the night. We'll teach you the basics of handling a sub and working the equipment."

"That would be fantastic! How soon can we do it?"

The admiral laughed. "Well, we'd better wait until you at least have the keel laid." This was a shipbuilding term which meant the actual start of construction on a new vessel.

The boys got home late that night and related the day's events to the Danfords. Mike's mother gasped as they told of the car chase, and his father's jaw went tight with barely concealed anger. But they all laughed when Josh described the look on Mike's face when the admiral had said the sub could go to fifteen hundred feet. When finally there was nothing more to tell, Mike's sister had a surprise for the boys.

"In honor of this great occasion, we have prepared a little celebration." She went into the kitchen and returned carrying a large cake in the shape of a submarine.

"Now you can have your cake, and sail it too!"

The next three weeks went slowly for Mike. School started again, limiting the number of hours he had to work on the sub. Besides trigonometry, chemistry, English and health, Mike was taking a class in ancient myths and mythology. One afternoon Josh walked into Mike's room and found him drawing on a huge piece of paper covering one whole wall.

"What's that?" Josh asked. "A design for your next submarine?"

"Funny, Josh. It's called studying, maybe you've heard of it? I have a test in Myths and Legends tomorrow."

Josh squinted at the lines on the paper and read out loud. "Titans, Olympians, Zeus, Athena, Pandora . . . what is all this?"

"A chart of all the different Greek gods. See, Uranus was the father of Cronus," Mike said, following the lines on the chart, "who was the father of Zeus, and so on."

"I didn't know gods had fathers," Josh said.

"They did in ancient Greece," Mike answered. "The Greeks believed in having a god for everything. Like Themis — he was the god of justice and order. Or Uranus, the god of the sky, which is why someone named one of our planets after him."

Josh screwed up his face, confused. "But these gods aren't *real*, are they?"

"Of course not," Mike laughed. "But it's still fun to study what they believed way back then."

"What's this one," Josh asked, pointing to the chart. "Pro — me — thee — us?"

"Prometheus," Mike repeated. "He's the god of wisdom and planning."

"That's nice, but I think I'll stick with the real God. Hey, want to come down to the beach with me?"

"Sorry, I've got to keep at this. I have to know all this stuff by tomorrow. Some of us actually have to study you know. We can't all run off and play with the little fishes all the time."

Mike was referring to a class in marine biology Josh was taking at a local college. Since Josh always got good grades, he was able to get special permission to take one college class each semester.

"You could stay and help, though!" Mike added.

Josh started backing out the door. "Uh, you know Mike, I'd love to, but I really do have to get to the beach. Someone has to hold down all that sand!"

Mike turned back to his studying with a laugh.

The good part of school starting was that it also brought the return of Jessica Kingston. Jessica was a sophomore with long brown hair and blue eyes. She had gone on vacation with her family during spring break, and Mike had missed her more than he expected. Though they were not officially going together, Mike really liked Jessica's company, and spent a lot of time thinking about her.

"Oh, Mike! You could have been killed!" she cried after hearing of the week's events. Mike didn't know which of the three incidents she was talking about, but he didn't much care. Her concern made him feel good inside.

"Yeah, I know," he answered as they ate their lunches in the school's outdoor courtyard. "Sometimes I just wish my dad could go with me everywhere and protect me. But I know he really can't. Guess I'm a little old for that anyhow."

"I don't think you're ever too old to need your parents," Jessica said. "But you're right that no one can protect you all the time."

"Guess I'll just have to leave it up to my guardian angel," Mike answered with a grin.

Mike felt good as he walked to his next class. I'm glad I shared my feelings, he thought. It's like a huge weight has been lifted off my chest.

Every day after school Mike and Josh, and sometimes Jessica, would spend hours tracking down parts for the submarine. The hardest part was the hull itself. It would be a steel pipe twenty feet long, seven feet high, and two inches thick. Only a major steel mill could handle a job this big.

The first two steel mills the boys called said they could do the work, but wanted more money than Mike had planned to spend on the whole submarine. Next they visited Stevenson Steel Corporation.

"Well, this doesn't look too difficult." Mr. Stevenson's rough face looked out of place in the fancy office overlooking the plant. Triple-paned glass kept out the noise and heat from the factory. The boys watched, fascinated, as tons of white-hot steel was poured from huge buckets into waiting molds.

"Stevenson Steel would be honored to help you with this project. You realize, however, that it will be expensive."

"Yes, sir," Mike replied. "About how much do you estimate it would cost?"

Stevenson quoted a figure that was much higher than either of the other two companies. Mike's chest tightened, but he tried to hide his disappointment.

"That, of course, is the full retail price for our regular customers." Mr. Stevenson's face melted into a smile. "For a partner, the price would be about one tenth that amount."

"Partners?" Mike could not conceal his excitement.

"That's right, partners. In return for at least one ride on the sub, and permission to use it in our advertising campaigns, Stevenson Steel would be glad to help foot the bill for your project."

"All *right!*" the boys yelled as they high-fived.

The two friends and Mr. Stevenson talked enthusiastically about the procedure for half an hour. A legal contract was drawn up for Mike's father to sign, and a date set for casting the hull. As they finished up the details, Josh's cell phone rang. He answered it, then handed it to Mike. "It's for you."

Mike was surprised. "Hello?"

"Mike! It's Jessica. Thank heavens I found you. You've got to get to the hospital quick. Your sister's been in an accident!"

It was a twenty-minute drive to the hospital in the city, and Josh made it in eighteen. He obeyed all the traffic laws, but just barely. All Jessica had been able to tell Mike was that she had come over to his house and found a note for him on the door. Apparently the Danford's didn't know which factory Mike was at, and couldn't get through on Josh's cell phone inside the steel mill. But Jessica kept trying until she connected. "The note just said your sister was in an accident, and that they'd call from the hospital," Jessica had said through the static on the phone.

Racing into the Emergency Room, Mike and Josh went straight to the busy admitting desk. "Danford! Do you have someone here named Danford?"

The overworked admitting clerk had long ago given up caring about other people's problems. She dragged her fingers over her keyboard and slowly punched up the right screen. "What's the first name?"

Mike stopped short as he realized he didn't know *which* sister to ask for. "Uh, I don't know."

The wrinkled face of the clerk stared back at him from beneath her white cap. "Look, kid, I've got fourteen patients to admit. I don't have time to play games."

"It's either Amy Rachelle or Katie Marie. I don't know which."

"Katie Marie Danford," she read back from the screen. "Room four-twenty-six."

"Thanks." Mike was too worried to notice the clerk's rudeness.

It only took minutes to find the room on the fourth floor, and as they entered they saw Mike's family standing around the bed. Katie, her jet black hair flowing over her shoulders, lay in the bed. A bandage covered her right hand and another her forehead. To Mike's relief, she was smiling.

"Mike! What are you doing here?"

"Sis, are you all right?"

"Sure. Its just a little burn. I keep telling them I don't need to stay here, but you know how doctors are. They think they know more about medicine than anyone else."

"Now Katie," her mother chided, "you know they need to keep you under observation in case there are any side effects."

"Side effects to what? What happened?" Mike asked impatiently.

Katie looked shyly around the room and said in obvious embarrassment,

"Well, I kind of blew up the chemistry lab at school."

Mike fell into a nearby armchair, doubled over in laughter. When he could finally talk he said, "That's worse than the time you set the home-ec kitchen on fire in high school!"

"All right, so I don't have a knack for cooking. Brownies *or* formulas. So *sue* me!"

Finally, Mike was able to control his laughter. "Seriously sis, how bad is it?"

"Not too bad. It's just a minor burn on the back of my hand and a small cut on my forehead. They think I might have inhaled some poisonous gas, though, so they want me to stay here overnight."

"I'd say you got off pretty easily, if that's the worst of it."

"That's *not* the worst of it," she replied. "I've been kicked out of chemistry!"

They stayed for a while longer, Mike telling the news about the Stevenson contract. Despite her insistence that she was fine, it was obvious that the accident had been hard on Katie. Seeing she was tired, Mike decided to leave.

"I guess Josh and I will take off, sis. I'll be back to see you tomorrow."

"Oh, you don't have to do that. They'll probably let me out right after breakfast."

"Breakfast?" The mention of food always got Josh's attention.

"Okay, Rover, let's go get some dinner." The others laughed as Mike led Josh out of the room by an imaginary leash.

Just before they went out the door Mike's dad called after them. "You boys are going straight home, right?"

"Well, I was thinking of stopping for a burger first, if that's okay." Mike was hungry too.

"All right, but then come right home." It was, as Mike was painfully aware, a school night.

"Sure, Dad," Mike answered, and then to Josh said, "Heel boy!" Josh made barking noises as he followed Mike out the door. Just then a cute blonde nurse walked by and gave Josh a funny look. He instantly blushed and tried to hide.

On the elevator the two friends talked about the time Josh had been in the hospital to have his tonsils removed. They got off at the first floor and started heading for the main entrance. As they passed a hallway Mike stopped dead in his tracks and grabbed Josh by the jacket.

"Josh," he whispered. "Look over there."

Fifty feet down the hallway a man dressed in a doctor's smock was coming out of a door marked Physicians Lounge. Josh instantly recognized the man. It was Elmer Baker, owner of the boat that had almost crushed Mike!

CHAPTER FOUR
INTERNET INTRUDER

Reacting swiftly, Mike pushed Josh into the nearest doorway, which happened to be a large library of medical books for doctors. Peeking through the almost closed door, Mike watched as "Doctor" Baker approached. Mike's heart lurched as he realized Baker was headed straight for them.

"Quick, get behind that shelf!" Mike was pointing to one of the many bookcases that filled the room. Josh started to protest, but Mike clamped a hand over his friend's mouth. "He's coming in here," Mike whispered urgently, releasing Josh.

"So what, why should we . . ." Mike had his hand over Josh's mouth again.

"Just play along with me, okay?"

Josh pulled Mike's hand away and whispered, "There's nothing wrong with doing right, Mike, and this feels very wrong!"

"Well it's not right that Baker's out to get me!" Mike hissed. "Now come on!"

Mike and his reluctant friend moved behind the bookcase just as Baker entered the room. Watching from between two books, the boys saw him go to a long row of shelves, select a book, and sit down to read. After a while he brought out a pad of paper and began taking notes.

Twenty minutes went by with no sign that Baker was planning to leave any time soon. Josh pointed to his watch, but Mike just shrugged. Baker was sitting at a table which was only six feet from the door and facing it. There was no way the boys could sneak past him. There were no other doors in the room, and all the windows were the kind that don't open. Resigning themselves to a long wait, the boys quietly sat down on the floor. Mike desperately wanted to dig out some Jolly Ranchers, but knew the sound of the wrappers would give them away.

Before long the floor was very uncomfortable. The library was carpeted, but that didn't help much. The deathly quiet of the place meant that he and Josh had to remain absolutely still. The smells from the cafeteria down the hall made their stomachs grumble.

I've got to find out what Elmer Baker's doing in a medical library, Mike thought, looking between some books at the handsome man in his mid-thirties. He doesn't look like a criminal, but I can't believe he's a doctor!

The minutes passed slowly for the two spies. At that time of night no other doctors came in to use the library, but neither did Baker show any sign of leaving. He had taken several pages of notes, and Mike was dying to know what he was writing.

Shortly after ten o'clock, more than three hours after he had sat down, Baker finally got up, stretched and returned the book to its shelf. Gathering his papers he went to a wall phone and pushed a single button.

"This is Doctor Boyd. I'll be leaving the hospital now."

Mike and Josh stared at each other, mouthing one word in unison. "*Boyd?*"

The doctor left and the boys stood up stretching and taking deep breaths. After three hours of trying to be quiet, they were exhausted.

"I can't wait to find out what he was reading," Mike exclaimed. He hurried over to the bookcase and pulled out the book the doctor had been using.

Mike looked at the title and his face fell. "Surgical Procedures for the Foot!" Mike thumbed through the book, looking at pictures of feet in various stages of surgery.

"What did you expect?" Josh asked. "It's a *medical* library."

"I know," Mike said, disappointed. "I was just hoping it was something more . . . suspicious."

"What's to be suspicious? The man is a doctor, Mike. He works in a big doctorly building doing all kinds of doctorly things. What did you expect to find?"

"You heard him on the phone. His name is *Boyd*, not Baker. Why should he lie about his name at the marina if he doesn't have anything to hide? I think he's up to something."

"I'll tell you what I think," Josh shot back. "I think he's just a very busy doctor who likes to get away and go fishing at a place where nobody will be able to find him. That's what I think."

Mike sighed. "Maybe you're right," he admitted, "but it sure seems funny. I want to make one more stop before we leave." If I can just get his address, Mike thought.

Mike led the way out to the main lobby and over to the information booth. As they approached, a pleasant older woman looked up from the book she was reading. "May I help you?"

Mike smiled back, trying to sound sincere. "I hope so. My sister was brought in here this afternoon from an accident . . ."

"Oh, I'm sorry to hear that."

"Thank you. She's going to be fine, thanks to the quick work of the doctor. In fact, he did such a good job fixing her up that I'd like to send him a thank-you note. The problem is I don't know the his address."

"Oh, that's easy," the woman replied. "Just send it to the hospital. They'll forward it to the doctor."

Mike felt the pang of disappointment, but decided he'd better finish the deception. "Could you give me the address here?" He wrote it down, then said, "Could you give me the doctor's first name? I'd like to make the note as personal as I can."

"Certainly. Which doctor is it?"

"Boyd. Doctor Boyd."

"That would be Doctor *Everett* Boyd," she said. "He's a wonderful man. Always very kind and gentle with his patients. No wonder you want to thank him. By the way, what's your sister's name, maybe I can look in on her?"

Not wanting anyone to know who he was, Mike decided he'd better not give his sister's real name. He stole a glance at the computer screen on the desk and used the name at the top.

"Pinkernell. Violet Pinkernell."

The receptionist gave Mike a funny look. "But, Violet Pinkernell is eighty-six years old. She's your *sister*?"

"Oh, uh, well, I didn't mean she was *really* my sister. I just meant she's . . . uh . . . my sister . . . in the Lord."

"Oh, I see."

Mike's body relaxed as he realized the woman had bought his story.

"Well, I guess we'd better get home," he added.

Suddenly, he and Josh looked at each other in shock. Both yelled at once, "*Home!*"

As they raced out to the car, Mike knew he was in hot water. He was supposed to have been home hours ago, and he hadn't even called.

When they got back to Seacrest, Josh dropped Mike off at his house.

"You sure you don't want to come in?" Mike asked, thinking his father would be less angry if Josh were there too.

"Are you kidding? Three hours late, spying on a doctor, and lying to an old woman? You're dead meat. I'll come by tomorrow and pick up the pieces."

"Thanks, friend," Mike said glumly. "Guess I can't blame you, though."

Mike walked in the front door of the house and, just as he had expected, his father was waiting for him in the living room.

"I hope you have a good explanation, young man."

"Uh, well I have an explanation, but I don't know how good you'll think it is."

"Try me."

Mike spent thirty minutes explaining the whole story to his father, from the "suspicious" boat, to the run-in with the doctor and the deception of the receptionist. Even as he told it, he felt the story was weak, but he knew from experience that lying to his father wasn't an option -- it only made things worse. When he had finished, Mr. Danford stood and paced the floor.

"Mike, I can see how you might think the boat was suspicious, but that doesn't excuse you from spying on Mr. Baker . . . Boyd. He has a right to his privacy. He's done nothing to you, except by accident, and what he does is none of your business."

Mike knew that what his father was saying was right, but still thought there was something more to it. "I just can't help feeling that Boyd had something to do with the motorcycle attack and the car that followed us. Those things happened right after the boat accident."

Mr. Danford considered this for a moment. "All right, Mike. I can understand how you might connect the three events. But the fact remains that, even after you got out of the library, you didn't call to tell us where you were. Also, you know it's wrong to lie. You had no reason for deceiving that receptionist. The fact that you didn't get the information you wanted, and got caught up in your own lies, shows that God had a good reason for outlawing them. There's just no excuse for it."

"Yes, sir. I mean no, sir." Mike felt frustrated, mostly with himself for doing such a dumb thing.

"I'm not going to punish you for being late. You had what you thought was a good reason. But for not calling you can apologize to your mother, and for lying you can call the receptionist and apologize."

"Yes, sir." Mike got up to leave, thinking he had gotten off pretty easy. But his father wasn't finished yet.

"And Mike..."

"Yes, sir?"

"You're grounded for a week."

"Yes, sir," he sighed.

The two apologies had been easy, but the week of grounding was agonizing for Mike. There were so many things to get done before construction on the sub could start. Finally, the week came to an end and he and Josh once again went on their search for sub parts. One evening found them at the Aerospace Surplus Store, where a giant airplane manufacturer sold used and left-over parts.

"Wow, look at all this stuff!" Josh had never been to the store, and what he saw overwhelmed him. The place was a huge warehouse with row after row of shelves. The shelves contained thousands of boxes of rivets, electrical connectors, nuts and bolts, plastic clips, and things Mike and Josh couldn't even begin to name. One whole side of the building held larger items such as electric motors, boxes of electronic equipment, desks, sheets of aluminum, and large racks of pipe. Just about anything the boys could want was in the store. As they walked up and down the aisles, Mike took careful notes on the various parts he thought he could use, and their price. At the end of one aisle Mike stopped, his face breaking into a grin.

"Josh, we've hit a gold mine!"

Sitting on a pallet were four slightly used but perfectly good pilot's seats from a jetliner. Though badly in need of new upholstery, the seats worked fine, moving up, down, back and forth on geared tracks.

"We'd better grab these today, before someone else gets them."

Along one wall of the complex were several shelves holding rolls of cloth used to cover airline seats. Mike selected a bright orange roll with wide red and brown stripes. "For the seats we found," he explained to Josh.

"Orange?" Josh moaned. "You're going to have orange seats?"

"It's the cheapest material they have," Mike explained. Josh was about to say he'd pay for some other color, but then he looked at the price tags and changed his mind.

After two hours of shopping, Mike paid for the seats and cloth, and the boys headed home with their finds in the back of Mr. Danford's pickup truck.

The next week and a half was busy. Between homework, youth group, the submarine plans, and working at the marina, Mike barely had time to sleep. As his nights got shorter he became more and more tired. Soon he quit reading his Bible and praying in the mornings. I just don't have time today, but I'll do twice as much tomorrow, he thought each day. But his Bible continued to lay untouched on his night stand.

"What's wrong with you?" Josh asked one day. "You've been grouchy all week."

"I'm *not* grouchy," Mike snapped. "I'm just getting sick and tired of your butting in . . ." Mike stopped short, shocked at what he was saying to his best friend. It was then that he decided he needed both his sleep *and* his devotion time.

"I'm sorry, Josh. I just forgot to do something important this morning." He explained the problem, then continued. "It's so hard for me to read the Bible every day," he confessed. "I really do want to read, but it seems like there's always something else to do. Then when I don't read my day ends up being rotten."

"I know what you mean," Josh said. "I have the same problem."

"Maybe we should start reading together," Mike suggested.

Josh thought about this for a moment then said, "Good idea. How about tomorrow morning?"

"You're on. Let's meet down by the water before school." Mike felt better just having made the decision.

Two days later Mike raced home to his computer right after school. Josh walked in half an hour later. Mike was staring intently at the computer screen.

"Hey! I've been looking all over for you."

Mike heard him but didn't answer.

"Mike? Hello Mike."

Mike was still too deep in thought. Suddenly he jumped up with a look of excitement. "That's *it*! I've got it!" Then finally realizing his friend was there said, "Josh! Where did you come from?"

Josh started to answer but Mike cut him off. "Never mind, it doesn't matter. What matters is I found the answer to our sweat problem."

Josh gave him a look of horror. "I didn't know I *had* a sweat problem!"

"Not you, the submarine."

"What a relief. For a minute there I thought I was going to be a social outcast."

"Very funny. I'm talking about the problem of the submarine sweating in cold water." Seeing that his friend didn't quite grasp it, Mike tried to explain.

"It's like when you have a glass of pop with ice in it on a warm day. The cold from the ice meets the warm moist air causing water droplets to form on the outside of the glass. On a dive, the cold from the water will do the same thing on the inside of the sub, making it very uncomfortable, if not dangerous."

"I get it. It would be like having our own rain machine inside the sub."

"Well, kind of. Anyhow, we'd definitely get wet."

"So how did you find the answer?"

Mike grinned. "I went to Admiral Norton's design page and asked it how to solve the problem."

"And . . ."

"And it told me to connect a dehumidifier directly into the main nuclear reactor and cool down then heat up the air."

"But you don't *have* a nuclear reactor."

"Exactly. So then I asked it to list other ways to get water out of the air and it gave several, including calcium chloride."

Josh was getting bored. "Okay, I'll bite. What's calcium chloride?"

"A chemical that removes moisture from the air and collects it wherever you want it. Once it turns the water vapor into liquid water, it stays water and won't evaporate. In fact, if you spill it on your clothes they'll never dry."

Josh's face lit up. "Hey, that would be great! I could use it on the lawn and never have to water it again!"

"It doesn't work that way. The calcium chloride would kill the grass."

"Even better! I'd never have to *mow* the lawn!"

"We're talking about submarines, remember?"

"Okay. So how do we use the stuff?"

"That's where the computer really helped. I used Admiral Norton's engineering program and came up with a small canister design that will fit right into the air-conditioning system." Mike was pointing to the computer screen. "The water will be drawn out of the air and drained into this plastic bottle . . ."

Suddenly, the drawings on the screen disappeared and were replaced an instant later by two flashing words: SECURITY ALERT! Below this a second message appeared: WARNING! UNAUTHORIZED TERMINAL MONITORING THIS LINE.

Mike gasped in horror.

"What does that mean?" Josh asked.

"It means someone's hacked into my computer!"

A moment later the warning dissolved and a new message appeared: FORMATTING HARD DRIVE.

CHAPTER FIVE
A DREAM COMES TRUE

Mike's fingers raced over the computer keyboard. Within seconds he commanded the computer to stop erasing the hard drive on his computer, but it was too late. The entire submarine file was gone.

"Now what are you doing?" Josh asked.

"I'm trying to get the computer to trace the hack back to its source. If I can't have my files, I at least want to know who does have them."

Several minutes passed as Mike worked quickly, giving the computer instructions and answering its questions. The phone rang downstairs and Mike's mother said that it was for him.

"Get that for me, will you Josh?"

"Sure thing." He returned a few minutes later. "That was Admiral Norton. He happened to be watching his computer terminal when he saw the security alert on the screen. He has the base security people checking it out."

"Well, I hope they have more luck than I did." Mike pointed to the screen which said simply, UNABLE TO TRACE. "They cut the connection before the computer could find them."

"How much did you lose?"

"Nothing, really. It's all backed up. But the bad part is that whoever did it e-mailed all my submarine plans to themselves before they were erased."

Mike called Admiral Norton, but the Navy security people had been just as unsuccessful as Mike.

"Obviously whoever hacked into your computer is an expert," the admiral said.

Mike unconsciously ran his finger around the buttons on the phone, wondering if he should mention Dr. Baker/Boyd. Finally he decided not to. But the old frustrations and fears were coming back, and he had to swallow hard to keep his voice from shaking. I can't take much more of this, he thought. Into the phone he said, "What I don't get is why anyone would want to hack into my computer in the first place."

"That is rather strange. Perhaps they just stumbled onto your computer by chance." It was obvious the admiral didn't really believe this.

"Whatever it was," Mike concluded, "I'm sure going to take some precautions from now on."

That night Mike lay in bed thinking about all that had happened since the boat accident. First the motorcycle attack, and being followed by someone in the green sedan. Then finding out that Elmer Baker was really Everett Boyd, and now having someone hack into his computer and erase his hard drive. Every thought made his insides feel more like a convention of worms.

He began to pray his usual prayer, but suddenly that wasn't enough. "God, help me," he cried into his pillow. "I'm so scared!"

With that the tears came and Mike poured out to God all the things that had built up inside. "I don't know who's after me, and I don't even know why. I'm scared just to walk down the street alone and I can't get to sleep at night." The more he prayed, the more he felt the tension drain from his body.

Sometime later, after telling God everything, Mike felt a lot better and a peace came over him. "Thank you Jesus," he prayed. "I know you are with me."

With that, he was sound asleep.

Three days later it was finally time for the Great Event. All day, Josh and Mike could think of nothing else. It seemed like time was standing still, leaving the boys stuck in seventh period. Even Jessica was anxious, as she too was looking forward to the Big Moment. The whole school knew about it, and everywhere kids were talking. Today was the day that Stevenson Steel was going to pour the hull for Mike's submarine.

Finally, the second hand on the clock ticked off the last thirty seconds of class and the bell rang. As if bitten by some unseen bug, Mike, Josh and Jessica all jumped up and headed for the door.

When they arrived at the Danford home, Mr. and Mrs. Danford and Amy were already waiting.

"Dad! What are you doing home?"

"You don't think I'd miss the Big Event, do you? I took the rest of the day off work so I could go with you."

Mike put his arm around his father's shoulders. "Thanks, Dad!"

The drive to the factory was full of joking and expectation. They arrived and Mr. Stevenson met them in the lobby. He gave them each a hard hat and ear plugs to wear.

Before entering the plant, Mr. Stevenson explained how the men and machines inside would form the hull. "The boat itself will be in three pieces," he said. "The main body will be a pipe twenty feet long, then a cone-shaped piece in the back, and a collar for the front. Mike and Josh will, of course, have to weld those two pieces to the body later."

Seeing that his audience understood this he continued. "Once we go inside the factory, it will be too noisy to hear very well. So remember any questions you have and I'll answer them when we're through. Are there any questions now?"

Josh was the first to speak up. "How long will it take?"

Mr. Stevenson considered this for a moment. "It should take about an hour, once we start to pour. We've been heating the steel all day and it will be ready as soon as we go in. They're waiting for word from me to start."

"Is this ordinary steel," Mr. Danford inquired, "or a special alloy?

"It's a special blend called HY150 that we've found to be particularly good for high pressure use in cold temperatures."

There were no other questions so Mr. Stevenson led the way. "If you'll follow me, we'll get started," he said with a smile.

They went down a long concrete hallway, then through two sets of heavy steel doors. The four who had never been to the plant gasped as they entered. The room was enormous, stretching out for hundreds of feet in every direction. The ceiling seemed a hundred feet high, and the sounds of dozens of pieces of heavy machinery echoed through the room. The air smelled like rotten eggs from the chemicals being used.

At one end of the building were four huge furnaces for melting the raw steel. Even with the large blowers in the ceiling, the room felt as hot as an oven.

Josh tried to say something to Mike, but the roar of the furnaces prevented any communication, and he soon gave up.

Mr. Stevenson led them to a platform from which they could see a set of large rollers on the floor, with strange-looking machines at each end. With a wave of his hand, Mr. Stevenson signaled the men in the control room high above, behind a glass wall, to start the operation.

A knot formed in Mike's stomach and he clenched the railing tightly. He had waited and planned and dreamed of this day for months. I can't believe it's really happening, he thought to himself.

The six watched as a giant bucket moved across the ceiling on a crane. The bucket descended into one of the furnaces and a few minutes later came out again, this time glowing red hot. The bucket slowly moved over to one of the machines at the end of the roller section. Gradually the fifteen-foot-wide bucket began to pour its contents into the top of the machine.

With sparks flying, the machine started up. Wheels spun, rollers turned, and in a few minutes a slab of steel began to squeeze out the bottom of the machine from between two rollers. The slab had perfectly straight sides, was about two inches thick, and was glowing red-hot.

When the slab was exactly the right length, a massive blade slammed down, cutting it off. The steel slab traveled down the set of rollers and into the second machine, which was a series of large wheels.

The group watched as each set of wheels curved the sides of the hot metal slab up a bit more, gradually forming it into the shape of a pipe. When it came out of the last set of rollers, the flat sheet of metal had been curved into a round pipe. Next, the pipe passed under an automatic welding machine which welded the seam closed. The pipe then went through a misty spray of water which caused an explosion of steam as the steel rapidly cooled. Several more stations inspected, trimmed and sized the pipe until it was finally declared to be perfect.

Next a crane lifted the pipe and carried it high in the air, across to a wooden framework built especially to hold it for transport.

Mike and Josh grinned at each other as they saw the completed hull section. Mike had trouble choking back tears of joy. What had been a dream for so long was finally becoming a reality!

The group watched as the crew repeated the entire process to form the cone-shaped aft section of the hull and the collar for the front. Finally, the steel workers made other minor parts and the ballast tanks. In less than an hour Mr. Stevenson led the group to his office where refreshments were waiting.

"Well, what do you think?" Mr. Stevenson asked.   "It was fantastic!" Mike didn't even try to hide his excitement. "There's hardly anything left to do!"

"Well, I wouldn't go that far," the steel man said with a laugh. "But I think we've given you a good start on the project. The rest is up to you."

The group talked excitedly as they finished the pop and chips Mr. Stevenson offered. Next came the task of transporting the sub parts. Mr. Danford had hired a tractor-trailer rig, and soon they had the frameworks holding the steel parts loaded and tied down.

The trip to the high school was slow but uneventful. Mr. Johnson, the shop teacher, gave a low whistle as the trailer backed into the bay of the shop.

"That's some piece of metal. How much does it weigh?"

"The center hull section is around thirty thousand pounds," Mike explained. "The rest of it is another four or five thousand."

Using a series of heavy-duty hydraulic jacks, they raised the main body of the submarine off the trailer. Then the trailer was pulled out and the hull set down on the waiting 'pontoons' which were the ballast tanks. The hull was delicately balanced on the two smaller pipes, so Mike and Josh immediately began welding the pieces together to form a solid unit.

"First we'll preheat the metal so the weld won't break loose when it cools," Mr. Johnson explained. He showed the boys how to attach the special heaters to the metal. "And we'll use HY 150 welding rod. Otherwise the weld may not hold under extreme pressure."

Two hours later the job was finally done. Mike's family and Jessica had left long before, and now the boys, Mike's father, and Mr. Johnson stood back admiring the finished work.

"It's a piece of art!" Josh said proudly.

The grey hull with its pontoons stood over nine feet tall. To those who had worked so hard on it, the mass of steel was beautiful. Mike had no trouble imagining what it would look like when finished.

After a few minutes, Mike grabbed a ream of computer paper and made a check mark.

"What's that?" Mr. Johnson asked.

"That's our Submarine Construction Checklist," Mike answered. "And we just completed step number one — weld pontoons to hull."

"How many steps are there?" Mr. Johnson asked.

Mike and Josh looked at each other a little dismayed. "Oh, about fifteen thousand," Mike answered.

As they all left, Mike carefully locked the sub in its bay, and then locked the building as well. He slept little that night, going over and over the next steps of construction. Excitement and anticipation, and a little bit of pride, were all mixed up inside him.

At school the following morning, dozens of kids filed through the shop to see the new arrival. Though some had trouble picturing it as a submarine, all were awed by the sheer size of the craft. Even Nick Travis was impressed.

"Nice going, Mike," he said. "Looks like you're really going to pull it off."

Touched by Nick's sincerity, Mike responded warmly. "Thanks, Nick. You can be one of the first to get a ride."

"Great!"

Mike determined to make friends with Nick no matter what everyone else thought.

That afternoon Mike called Admiral Norton and told him of the sub's progress.

"That's wonderful, Mike. I'm looking forward to seeing it. By the way, when are you and Josh coming over to spend a couple days with us for some training?"

"Any time you're ready, I guess. It'll have to be on a weekend."

"How about this Friday and Saturday? The regular Navy classes will be on leave but the instructors will be here. It would be a perfect time to do a little training on the side."

"I'll talk to my parents, but I don't think it will be a problem," Mike replied.

"Excellent. Also, we've been scrapping out some old World War II ships down at the yard. I thought you might be able to use some of the parts off them."

"Super! I haven't been able to find a hatch or portholes yet."

"I'm sure we could help you out with that," the admiral said. "We'll take a look when you get here. I'll have to charge you, since it's government property. But the scrap value isn't very high so it shouldn't put too big a dent in your budget."

"Great," Mike said, already thinking of the possibilities. "I'll see you on Friday."

Nothing more could be done on the sub for the next two nights since Mike had to work after school. Even at the marina, though, the talk was mainly about Mike's plan. Jordan was particularly interested in Mike's progress, and when he heard that construction had actually begun he had a surprise for the young builder.

"Mike, I was thinking the other day that, once that sub of yours is finished, you're going to need a place to store it."

Mike looked at his boss suspiciously. "Yeah, so . . . ."

"So I've decided to let you keep it here, free of charge."

"Jordan, that's nice of you," Mike said, "but where?" The marina is full, and there's a waiting list a mile long. There's no space anywhere!"

"Follow me," Jordan said, leading the way to his office. "You know all those meetings I've been going to? Well here's what they were about." He unveiled a large drawing of the marina, showing a new section added on. "I present to you the new, expanded, Seacrest Marina. We're going to add on a whole new section at the north end. And right here," he said pointing to one part of the first floor, "is going to be this state's first privately owned submarine slip."

Mike stared at the drawings in disbelief. He had often wondered how he could get the sub to and from the water, but had decided he'd figure that out when the time came. With this new design he could lift the sub inside the marina and store it safely.

"I don't know what to say, Jordan, except thanks!"

"No problem, Mike. I've just been so impressed with your dedication to this project that I wanted to do my part to help you. I was going to add on to the marina anyway, and this feature won't cost that much more. Plus it'll be good publicity."

Mike spent twenty minutes studying the blueprints. He was curious about every detail of the plan. He finally went back to work, hardly believing the generosity of his boss.

A few hours later Mike was up on the third floor of the old wooden building, quickly cleaning the bottom a boat. A storm was approaching outside, and Mike wanted to get home before it hit the marina.

He had just finished scrubbing the green slime and was starting to rinse off the hull when he heard the boat elevator arrive. He looked over, then felt his knees go weak. Standing next to a brand new cabin cruiser was Doctor Boyd, alias Elmer Baker!

Mike dropped the hose he was holding and ducked behind the nearest boat, but not before Boyd had seen him. Peeking around the bow of the boat, Mike saw Boyd reach for a bulge under his jacket.

Frantically Mike scanned the room. There was no one else there, and Boyd stood between him and the only exits. There was no escape.

Glancing back at the elevator Mike saw Boyd coming directly toward him. Boyd's face was cold and expressionless. His heart pounding, Mike froze in terror. He knew without a doubt that he was about to face death!

Drops of sweat broke out on Mike's face and neck as Boyd inched closer. Forcing himself to move, he crept behind the stern of the boat that was hiding him. Squeezed in between the wall and the boat's propeller, he found himself facing the name painted on the back of the boat: Double Devil. That name alone stabbed another knife of fear into his chest.

From his position behind the boat, Mike could move either left or right. He agonized for a moment, then decided to go right, toward the elevator end of the building.

He could no longer see Boyd, and the whistling of the wind through the old building covered the sound of Boyd's footsteps. The storm was fast approaching, and rain pelted the tin roof of the building.

Mike crouched down and moved slowly along the line of boats. He considered hiding inside one of the cruisers, but decided that would only be a temporary solution: sooner or later, Boyd would find him. So he kept moving, and when he reached the other end of the building he crept up between two speedboats. The stairway next to the elevator was only twenty feet away. If I can only get across there before he shoots, Mike thought.

Finally Mike decided to run for it. Rising slowly, but still hidden, he peeked around the bow of the boat on his left. Boyd was nowhere in sight. Wanting to move but afraid to, he felt like his feet were nailed to the floor. Mike's heart pounded. His mouth was dry, and his whole body was drenched in sweat. He had never been so scared in his life! It was as if the whole world had shrunk to one small tunnel between him and the door to safety.

Mike told himself he'd run on the count of three. Forcing himself, he counted silently, his heart beating faster with every count. One . . . two . . . *three!* His left foot moved forward.

At that moment a hand grabbed his shoulder from behind. Spinning around, Mike stared into the cold, grey shark-eyes of Everett Boyd.

"Hey kid, is your name Mike?"

Mike could only stare back in horror.

"Must be, you're the only one up here." With his free hand, Boyd reached inside his coat again. Mike's heart lurched and his insides turn to jelly as he saw Boyd pull his hand out. A flash of steel was the last thing Mike saw as his world went black.

CHAPTER SIX
DISAPPOINTING DISCOVERY

"Mike! Wake up Mike." The voice was that of his boss, Jordan Washington.

"Wha - what happened?" Mike groggily opened his eyes and saw Jordan and Jake standing over him, concern on their faces. Mike gave a start as he saw a third face hovering above. Holding Mike's right wrist and taking his pulse was Doctor Everett Boyd!

"You passed out, son. I guess I startled you. My name is Elmer Baker. I was just bringing in my new boat and needed some help moving it. I didn't want to take any chances of it getting away from me again."

Mike sat up, still shaking. Jordan explained what had happened. "I sent Mr. Baker up here with this new lock for his storage shed."

Mike saw for the first time what Boyd had pulled out of his jacket: a large combination lock with a long shaft. "I told him you were up here and would help him move it, since only employees can move boats now. When you passed out he used the intercom to call me."

Mike's face turned from pale white to bright red as he realized what a fool he'd made of himself. "Uh, I guess I haven't been getting enough sleep lately."

"That's all right," Boyd said with a smile. "I'm just sorry my boat almost hit you the other day. I hope you're feeling better."

Mike forced himself to smile back, then sat on the floor recovering while Jordan and Jake helped Boyd move the new boat in. As before, the special dolly Boyd was using hid the bottom half of the boat.

I can't believe I fainted, Mike thought. How humiliating! I must really be blowing things way out of proportion.

With the boat safely locked in its shed, the others returned and helped Mike down to the office. After a glass of orange juice, he felt much better. Boyd and Jake left, leaving Mike and Jordan alone in the office. "You'd better take some time off," Jordan said. "I think you've worn yourself down."

"That was just a cover-up," Mike said, leaning forward. "I blacked out because I thought I saw Boyd pulling out a gun."

Jordan listened as Mike told the whole story.

"Everett Boyd? Why would he lie about his name?"

"I don't know, Jordan," Mike said quietly, shaking his head. "Josh thinks he just likes his privacy, and maybe he's right. It's just all so strange."

"Well, I can't say for sure of course, but I tend to agree with Josh. I don't doubt anything you say, but maybe you're just adding it up all wrong."

Mike let out a big sigh. "Maybe so. But do me a favor. Next time you send BakerBoyd around, warn me first."

Jordan laughed. "Sure Mike. I'm sorry I scared you like that. If I'd known, I sure wouldn't have sent him up there alone."

It was time for Mike to get off work and he went straight home. After calling Josh, he told his parents what had happened, and about all his fears. Mr. Danford, too, thought all the events were unrelated.

"I don't know whether to feel scared or just stupid," Mike told his father.

"How about neither?" Ben Danford replied. "With all you've been through you don't need to feel stupid about being a little suspicious. And the Bible assures us we don't need to live in fear if we trust the Lord."

Mike knew his father was right, and he really did want to trust God. But sometimes the fear beats out the faith, he thought.

The next day was Friday, so Mike and Josh left for Keyport right after school. Admiral Norton met them at the gate and escorted them to the BOQ — Bachelor Officer Quarters — where unmarried officers assigned to the base were housed. The room they were given reminded them of a modern hotel. "Not bad," Josh commented. "We even have our own TV!"

After dinner, the boys met the two men who would be their instructors. "Gentlemen," Admiral Norton said to the boys, "I'd like you to meet Captains Morris and Talbot. They'll be your instructors for the next twenty-four hours."

Mike liked the two Navy men from the start. Both looked professional in their crisp uniforms, but they were still casual and friendly with the boys.

The captains first led Mike and Josh to the submarine training center. For the first two hours, Captain Morris went through the basics of how a sub works. The boys drank in everything the officer said about buoyancy control, diving angles, air-regeneration and emergency procedures.

Next, Captain Talbot took them to the mock-up of an actual sub. Although nothing like Mike's sub, the two craft did have one thing in common: a periscope. For half an hour Mike and Josh learned the art of using the "scope", measuring distances and scanning the horizon for "bogies", "enemy" aircraft and boats. "It's a good idea to check the scope before you surface," Captain Morris said with a grin. "It's really embarrassing to come up right under another boat."

Mike wondered if the Captain knew this from experience, but didn't ask.

"This is great," he exclaimed as he looked through the periscope. "I'd swear we were on a real sub!"

After another hour of classroom work on sea currents and underwater navigation, the two students returned to their room for the night.

"Mike, even if we never finish your sub, this weekend will be worth all the work!"

"We're going to finish it, but you're right," Mike said, as they crawled into twin beds. "This is the experience of a lifetime."

They spent the next day learning the use of various types of equipment aboard a submarine. The boys learned about everything from depth sounders to air-conditioning systems. Then, after lunch, Captain Morris led them to another building.

After working their way through three security check points, they entered a small, dimly-lit room. Several sailors sat at consoles in the room, each wearing a pair of headphones. A large map of Admiralty Sound and the Pacific Ocean covered the front wall of the room, projected by a computer. Red, blue and green symbols flashed on the screen.

"Since we're going to talk about sound waves next," Captain Morris explained, "I decided there was no better place to learn than in our hydrophone center."

"What kind of phone?" Josh asked.

"A hydrophone," Mike answered. "It's a device for listening underwater."

The captain moved over to the projected image of the map. "These red dots show the location of underwater microphones we have planted all over the sea floor." Several dots made a line across the entrance to Admiralty Sound, and at other strategic points in the area.

"It's like sonar," Mike explained to Josh.

"Yes, that's exactly right," the captain said. "Except that the microphones are permanently anchored to the bottom of the sound, instead of housed on the side of your submarine. In any case, by listening through these remote microphones, we can hear anything that moves in the water. The trick is to identify what the sound is just by listening, and that's what this seaman is going to teach you." Captain Morris pointed to a sailor sitting at one of the consoles.

For two hours the boys learned how to tell the difference between a freighter and a pleasure boat, a single-propeller boat from a twin-propeller boat. They listened to ferries and fishing boats, tug boats and hydrofoils.

At one point Josh heard a strange crying sound. "What's that?" he asked. "Sounds like a sick seagull."

The seaman flipped a switch from Headphones to Speaker so they could all hear. "Oh, that's a 'biologic.'" Mike and Josh both looked at him blankly. "A biologic," the seaman repeated, "something *biological*, something *alive*. In this case a pod of killer whales," he said. Finally the boys understood, then got excited.

"I'm glad you got to hear this," the seaman continued. "They travel through the Sound all the time, and you'll no doubt run into them eventually." They tracked the whales for more than an hour, the computer showing their progress on the main chart.

Following their sonar training, Mike and Josh learned how to identify buoys and lighthouses, and then all about radios and what frequencies to use in an emergency. Late in the afternoon, Admiral Norton picked the boys up and took them to the base's scrap yard. On the way, they passed an enormous nuclear submarine receiving its final fittings.

"That's the Nebraska," the admiral explained. "She's the first of our newest class of submarine, design just specifically for fighting terrorist. They'll be launching her in just a few weeks."

I'd love to get a ride in that baby, Mike thought. The black hull seemed as long as two football fields, and rose six stories into the sky.

At the scrap yard they found a hatch, eight portholes and several gauges that Mike could use in his sub. After making arrangements for payment and saying their goodbyes, the boys drove home.

"Why do we need those gauges?" Josh asked. "I thought the whole thing was going to be computerized."

"It is," Mike answered. "We're building a computer into the console that will tell us everything, like how much pressure is left in the tanks, how the motors are performing — stuff like that. Just like a jet airliner. But — also like a jet airliner — we'll have real, metal-and-glass gauges as backups. Just in case the computer crashes."

"A computer crash!" Josh gasped. "That's *impossible!*"

Mike laughed at his friend's sarcasm. "Just the same, we'll build in some backups."

During the next two weeks work on the sub progressed at a fast pace. Mike would explain the blueprints to Josh, who then did most of the welding. One day Jessica came by to help, but Mike couldn't think of anything for her to do. He scanned the checklist and finally suggested she do one of the last steps, number 14,227 -- wash the glass on the portholes. Jessica looked at the list, then picked up a five-eighths-inch box end wrench. "How about I do step 8,942 instead," she said. "Install the hydraulic pump?"

Mike just gulped and looked shocked that she'd even know what a hydraulic pump was.

"My dad's a rancher," she said with a grin. "I help him work on the tractors all the time." She patted the still-shocked Mike on the back and said, "Just because I'm a girl doesn't mean I don't know a screwdriver from a socket wrench, you know." Mike blushed, and decided to never underestimate Jessica again.

Mike and Jessica moved the pump into place, then Jessica began bolting it down. As she did, Mike explained to her and Josh. "Under the floor plates will be the batteries, air tanks and hydraulic systems."

"Hydraulic systems? What are they for?" Josh asked. "I don't remember those in the original plans."

"They weren't," Mike answered. "Admiral Norton suggested them. All the steering systems will be hydraulically operated . . . like a bulldozer. That way, no matter how strong the current is, we'll be able control the sub's movement. Or so the theory goes."

"What's above the ceiling?" Jessica asked.

"The air recycling unit and all the electronic equipment."

The boys worked furiously every night after school, except when Mike had to work at the marina. In no time at all they had the floor and ceiling in place. Josh cut a hole on top of the hull for the hatch, and another one for the periscope. Four more holes along each side were made for the portholes. Meanwhile, Mike began the tedious job of constructing the banks of valves that would control the air supply system.   Jessica stopped by to check on progress one night, and Mike was more than glad to see her. She watched as he carefully connected several chrome-plated valves together.

"There are a total of eight large tanks of compressed air," he explained. "These will be used for blowing the water out of the ballast tanks, and for adding oxygen into the breathing system when necessary." Mike tightened each fitting with an open-end wrench. "With these valves we can route the air to any place we need it."

Mike's father, some of his other friends, and Mr. Johnson also helped whenever they could. In fact, the whole school had become excited about the project, and a contest was held to name the craft. Mike chose the winning entry, but said he wouldn't announce it until the launch of the sub.

Even Mrs. Danford and Amy got involved, cutting the hundreds of pieces of colored wire that were needed, and bundling them together.

One Saturday the mass of steel finally started looking like a submarine when the crew built and welded in place the conning tower on top of the sub. Standing three feet high and five-feet long, the tower was pointed at each end and bulged out in the middle. The hatch was installed on top of the tower, and the periscope hole cut directly in front of that. A ladder was installed down through the main hull and into the cabin. In the front of the tower was another round compartment about a foot deep.   "What's that for?," one of Mike's friends asked.

"That will hold the emergency locator buoy. If we get into trouble, we can release the buoy from inside the sub. It will float to the surface and automatically send out an emergency radio signal. It also will have a strobe light so they can find it at night."

It was getting harder and harder for Mike to be patient. Each new addition to the sub made him that much more anxious to get it finished and in the water. Every night he'd lie in bed dreaming about what it would be like to dive below the surface of Admiralty Sound.

Late one night Mike was working at his computer when his father came into the room. "Hi. What are you working on?"

"Finances, Dad. I'm just checking how much money I've spent and how much more I need."

"How does it look?"

"Terrific," he said sarcastically. "I have enough to buy everything except the Plexiglass bubble. That gives me a very nice submarine with a five-foot hole in the front."

Mike leaned back in his chair and sighed. "I had hoped to launch just after school is out. Now I guess I'll have to wait a couple more months to save up enough money. Maybe Jordan will give me some more hours at the marina."

"How much will the bubble cost?" his father asked.

"I called several places today and they all said the same thing. It's about three hundred dollars more than I had planned on."

"That's too bad, son. I know it's hard to be patient, but you'll get there eventually."

"Yeah. I just hope I'll still be young enough to enjoy it!"

Two more weeks passed and the sub grew. Josh spent his time installing the steering mechanisms in the cone-shaped aft section, using rubber buffers to keep the hydraulic pipes from vibrating against the hull. Meanwhile Mike constructed the delicate electronic circuits that would help navigate, check the depth of the water below, and monitor the air in the sub for poisonous gases.

Several days were spent just in building the periscope. Though simple in theory, it was actually very complex and hard to install. "It works!" Mike yelled when he finally looked through it for the first time. "It really works!" Crouched inside the hull, he swung the periscope around looking at the ceiling of the shop, imagining what the view would be like from underwater.

A few evenings later Mike and Josh were just finishing connecting some hydraulic hoses when there was a loud banging on the garage door of the shop. Mike opened it and saw a flatbed truck with a large crate on it. An impatient delivery man stood there with a clipboard.

"You Mike Danford?" he asked abruptly.

"Uh, yes I am."

"Sign here." The delivery man pushed the clipboard at Mike, pointing to an 'X' on the form.

"What's this for?" Mike asked. "I didn't order anything."

"Look, kid, I don't explain 'em, I just deliver 'em. This here form says I'm to deliver this here crate to Mike Danford at this here address, and that's what I'm doing. You gonna sign or not?"

Without a word, Mike signed the form and they unloaded the crate. The driver tore off a copy of the form and handed it to Mike, then walked back to his truck and drove away.

"What do you think it is?" Josh asked.

"Only one way to find out," Mike replied. With that, he took a crowbar and started prying off the cover of the crate. Inside they could see nothing but Styrofoam packing. They started scooping out the chips of plastic and a moment later Mike gasped. Inside was a crystal clear, five foot Plexiglass bubble.

"I thought you couldn't afford this," Josh said in astonishment.

"I can't," Mike whispered back. "I don't even know where it came from."

"Maybe I can answer that." The voice from behind them startled the boys. They turned and saw Mike's mother and father entering the shop. "I guess we're too late for the unveiling," Ben Danford continued.

"Dad! What . . . where . . ." Mike felt totally confused.

"Well, your mother and I decided that you'd worked so hard on this project that you deserved a little help. So I ordered this for you a couple weeks ago."

"Mom, Dad. What can I say . . . except, thanks! It's beautiful!"

They finished unpacking the bubble. Made of two-inch thick plastic, it looked like the eye of a giant squid, and would be the front "windshield" of the sub. The four stood back admiring the bubble as it sat on the pallet.

"How does it attach to the sub?" Mike's mother asked.

"This lip on the inside edge of the bubble will bolt to a matching steel lip on the sub. A rubber seal between them will keep them water-tight."

They stayed a while longer, looking at the latest additions to the boat, then Mike's parents took him and Josh out for pizza.

Half the school passed through the shop the next day to see the new bubble. Everyone commented on its size and shape. It really is beautiful, Mike thought.

Since it was Wednesday, the boys had to quit working early that evening to go to their weekly church youth group meeting. They arrived a few minutes early and stood talking to their friends. As usual, the topic eventually came around to the submarine.

"How long until it's finished?" one of Mike's friends asked.

"Well, we're hoping it'll be done about the time school's out. That gives us three weeks."

A few minutes after seven the youth-leader gathered them in a circle and they began. The leader had talked Mike into leading the Bible study and, since it was his first time, he was nervous. His throat tightened up until it felt like a big hand was clamped around his windpipe. Once he started, though, his nervousness disappeared.

"I thought it would be only appropriate if tonight we studied the story of Jonah and the Whale."

The group burst into laughter. "Of course," one guy yelled. "We should have known."

Despite the humor of the group, the discussion was deep and serious.

"So Jonah told God he would do anything God wanted him to," Mike concluded a half-hour later, "as long as it was what Jonah wanted." Mike shifted his position while he chose his next words.

"Sometimes I find myself doing the same thing, telling God my life is His, as long as I get my own way. But I've really been finding out lately that faith in God means putting my life in His hands and accepting whatever He says, even if it's not exactly what I had planned." The group was silent as Mike continued.

"I don't want to be like Jonah was, rebellious and disobedient. I want to be like Paul, after he became a Christian. I want to have the courage to read the Bible, pray and talk about God to anyone anytime."

Mike dropped his gaze to the floor and finished quietly. "I have to admit that I haven't been very good at that so far. Sometimes I even feel a little embarrassed to talk about God. But I'm going to try to change that."

The group talked for a while, closed in prayer and then broke up for snacks. While talking to Jessica, Mike suddenly remembered something. "I was in such a hurry to get here," he said, "that I left the welder on back at the shop!"

Excusing himself, he said goodnight to his friends and headed back to the school. Mr. Johnson had given him a key to the shop, and he now used it let himself in.

As soon as he entered the door, Mike sensed that something was wrong. The room was dark, where usually one light was left on. And there was an acid smell in the air that reminded him of the time he threw some plastic forks into a campfire. He edged over to the light switch and, when he had flicked it on, cried out in shock.

Still on the pallet, his beautiful Plexiglass bubble had melted into a blob of blackish molten plastic. Mike walked over to it and, as he approached, detected the distinct odor of hydrochloric acid.

Mike's heart sank as he stared at the still-smoking mound of plastic. A moment later he jumped as a case of tools behind him smashed to the floor. A dark figure sprang from behind a shelf and sprinted to the light switch.

Knives of terror stabbed Mike's insides as the room plunged into blackness, the unknown attacker hiding somewhere in the dark.

CHAPTER SEVEN

A FRIGHTENING MESSAGE

"Who's there?" Mike demanded.

Silence.

"Who's *there*!?"

Mike swallowed hard, trying to force himself to think. He wanted to panic, but knew his only hope was to keep a clear head. He tried to picture what was near him in the room. He was standing at the front of the sub, next to the garage door. The door was locked and Mike didn't have a key for it.

"I have a fire axe!" Mike hoped his lie would stall the intruder.

Fear was taking over his mind. There was no mistaking it this time -- Mike was in real danger. Forcing himself to concentrate, an idea struck him, and he moved slowly to the other side of the sub.

Mike froze instantly when he heard the squeak of a shoe a few feet to his right. He waited a moment, then continued moving as quietly as a cat, feeling along the workbench.

"I'm sick and tired of you, Danford!" The hissing voice shot out of the dark like a bullet. "You're *dead*! You've been in my way for weeks, and now I'm going to get rid of you!" The voice didn't sound human. It was low and ugly, like some awful monster.

At last Mike found what he had been feeling for. His heart was pounding like a jackhammer, and sweat made his hands slippery. "Who are you?" he yelled, trying to keep the attacker talking. "What did I ever do to you?" If he could just stall for a few more seconds . . . .

"Shut up!" the voice squeaked. Mike jumped when he heard how close it was. "You have no idea how much trouble you've caused me!"

"I don't know what you're talking about!" Mike's hands were shaking so badly he had trouble turning the wheel. "What have I ever done to you?" Almost there . . . just one more turn.

"You know very well, Danford. And now you're going to pay for it!"

In that instant Mike squeezed the trigger that lit the gas welding torch. At the same time he pulled the fire alarm on the wall next to him. There was a scream as the flame of the torch hit the assailant square in the face.

That moment of light revealed that the intruder was wearing the same black outfit as the motorcycle rider, except that the helmet was replaced by a ski mask.

The attacker covered his eyes, stumbling backwards out of the torchlight. The horn of the fire alarm screaming was terrifying all by itself. A moment later Mike saw the door to the shop open and the figure run out into the moonlight.

Breathing heavily, Mike scrambled for the light switch and, as the lights flickered on, he locked the door. After making sure he was alone he went back to the torch, which he had thrown on the floor, and turned it off.

A few minutes later he heard the fire trucks arrive, then there was a pounding on the door. Mike opened it to the surprised look of Captain Washington. The firefighters found the alarm shutoff, and a few minutes later Mike had explained the whole thing to the Captain.

"That was a smart move, Mike," Captain Washington said. "Are you okay?"

"Yeah, thanks Cap. I'm just a little shaken up."

One of the firefighters had called the police and Mike's parents. School officials were automatically called by the fire department dispatcher.

Half an hour later the Danfords and Mr. Johnson stood looking at the melted Plexiglass bubble. A police officer was just finishing his report.

"Offhand I'd say the intruder had planned to do much more damage than he did, but you interrupted him."

"I think you're right, officer." It was Mr. Johnson. "After pouring the bottle of hydrochloric acid on the bubble, he apparently planned to try smashing the valve assembly and other critical parts." He pointed to a large sledge hammer which had been removed from its place on the wall and now lay on the floor nearby.

Mike knelt down and touched the only smooth part left on the bubble. "It was so cool," he sighed.

"Don't worry, Mike," Mr. Johnson said. "I'm sure the school insurance policy will cover it."

Mike was beginning to know police report forms better than some police officers. After signing this one he drove home with his parents.

"I think we'd better go have a talk with someone at the police department tomorrow," his father said. "This has gone too far."

"I agree, Dad, but what can the police do? There are no suspects, except Doctor Boyd, and no evidence even if they *had* a suspect."

Mrs. Danford broke into the conversation. "Well we've got to do *something!* I've met enough insane people in my day to know they can be dangerous!"

"But I can't stay locked in my room, Mike said. "I think all we can do is use common sense, and then trust God to take care of me."

Mike's parents couldn't argue this, and decided they could do nothing more than make sure Mike was always with someone. The most obvious choice was Josh.

"All right then, it's settled," Mr. Danford said. "You don't go anywhere alone. If Josh can't go with you, find someone else, but never go anywhere alone!"

Mike's parents talked to the police the next day but, as expected, there wasn't much to go on. The police did say they had already stepped up patrols around the Danford house and the school.

Despite the vandalism, work on the sub proceeded quickly. Within a few days they had joined the cone-shaped aft section to the main hull. Mike and Josh formed a pair of rudders out of reinforced fiberglass. Each rudder had a pod molded into it to hold one of the electric motors.

Two diving planes – little wings – were also formed, exactly like the rudders but without the motor pods. These were installed on the sides of the cone and would make the sub go up or down.

Saturday afternoon Mike asked Josh to go for a ride with him.

"Where to?" his friend asked suspiciously.

"You'll find out."

"Is this going to get me in trouble?"

"Probably."

Josh sighed. "Oh well, if I'm going to live like your shadow, I might as well get used to trouble. Give me a Jolly Rancher and lead the way."

They got in Josh's car and he started the engine. "Where to, oh master?"

"Valley General Hospital."

"Oh no," Josh cried. "You're not gonna spy on the Doc again are you?"

"I just want to ask a few questions, that's all. Drive on, and I'll explain."

Josh reluctantly did as his friend asked.

"It dawned on me today, while I was watching you weld, that I must have hurt whoever was in the shop the other night. My eyes watered just watching you for a second from fifteen feet away. The other night that guy was only a few feet away, so he must have had a flash burn."

"So you're gonna ask around the hospital and see if ole Doc Boyd had a bad case of redeye this week. Is that it?"

"Precisely, Mr. Roberts."

"What are you going to say? 'Excuse me, could you give me the time and, by the way, did Doctor Boyd receive any flash burns this week'?"

Mike laughed. "Yes, I thought that would be the best approach. Seriously, I don't know what I'll say. I'll figure that out when we get there."

The boys spent over an hour at the hospital, casually talking to nurses. They left, dejected, with only one possible conclusion: Doctor Everett Boyd definitely did not have a flash burn, and had not been absent from the hospital for a single day.

"Now will you *please* get off Boyd's case?" Josh pleaded as they drove home. "You've been suspecting him for two months without a shred of evidence, except that he likes his privacy."

"Yeah, okay," Mike finally conceded. "I guess you've been right all along. Boyd's not our man."

Josh was suddenly solemn. "Boyd may not be," he said, "but whoever it is, they're following us again."

Mike sat up and looked behind them. A dark maroon two-door Ford was a quarter mile behind. "What makes you think they're following us?"

"Trust me, I'm getting to be an expert at this."

"That does it!" Mike shouted. "I'm sick of this. We're going to find out who this is once and for all. As soon as we crest that hill, slam on the brakes and block the road."

"Do *what?*"

"Don't argue, just do it."

When they had climbed the hill and were out of sight on the other side, Josh did as Mike had instructed. Locking up the brakes and spinning the wheel, he stopped the car across both lanes of the road. In a flash Mike jumped out, grabbing a tire iron from behind the seat, and sprinted to a tree by the road. Josh dove into the bushes on the other side of the highway.

When the tailing car came over the hill Mike could see two men in the front seat. Shocked by Josh's sudden maneuver, the driver of the car slammed on the brakes, just barely stopping in time.

Before the driver could do any more, Mike sprang to the passenger side of the car, threatening the occupants with the tire iron. Josh took his cue from Mike and guarded the driver, holding a big stick he found on the side of the road.

"All right, this is it!" Mike roared. "I've had enough of this. Who are you and what do you want?"

The passenger started to reach inside his coat. "*Hold it,*" Mike shouted, "or you'll be dog food. Answer my question *now!*"

"Wait a minute, Mike, you're making a mistake. Just let me reach inside my coat and I'll show you who we are."

"All right," Mike said suspiciously, "but do it slowly."

The man reached in his jacket and pulled out a black wallet. Flipping it open, he displayed an identification card. "We're from Naval Intelligence. Admiral Norton assigned us to keep an eye on you after your father told him all that's been happening."

Mike lowered the tire iron. He could feel the blood rushing to his face in embarrassment. "Oh no." He stepped back, letting the man open his door.

"Hey guys, I'm sorry. I didn't know who you were and I just figured . . . well, anyhow, I'm sorry."

"Don't be, Mike. If anything, *we* should be sorry. We're supposed to be highly trained bodyguards, and here you get the drop on us like we're a couple of boy scouts."

A thought suddenly occurred to Mike. "How long have you been tailing us, anyhow?"

"Since the day after the attack at the shop. Between us and the other agents, we've been your constant companions. By the way, that's a cute girlfriend you have."

Mike blushed again. "Uh, thanks. She's not really my girlfriend, we're just kinda friends."

That night Mike told his father about the trip to the hospital. "I wasn't spying on Doctor Boyd, honest, Dad. And I didn't lie. I just asked a few questions and gained a few facts, that's all. I just had to know."

"Well, I can't blame you, son. It must be hard having someone after you and not know who it is. At least you've eliminated Doctor Boyd as a suspect. And you didn't lie to anyone?"

"No sir. I just asked a few people if Doctor Boyd had been in this week and if he seemed okay. I didn't make up any stories about why I wanted to know."

"In that case, I can't see that you did anything wrong. I am surprised, though, about the Navy men. I didn't know that Buck . . . Admiral Norton . . . would send out bodyguards. I'm glad he did, though. I feel much better."

"Me too. The guys said Admiral Norton was using the intrusion into his computer as an excuse to have the Navy protect me while they investigate. Anyhow they're here, and that's the important part."

The submarine was almost finished. Another week had gone by, and only one was left until school would be out for the summer. Most of the controls were now installed in the boat, as well as the portholes, batteries and air tanks.

During the last week of school the boys installed the control column in front, and put the finishing touches on the sub, including the seats. Mr. Johnson had ordered the new bubble, but it had not yet arrived.

With five days left of school, Mike and Josh masked off the portholes and other openings, and started applying coats of primer and yellow paint to the hull. The paint made a big change in the appearance of the sub. It's just like I imagined, Mike thought with a smile.

On the last day of school both boys were called out of their second period class and told to report to the shop. When they arrived, Mr. Johnson proudly stood next to an already un-crated plastic bubble. "It's exactly like the first," he said. "Perfect!"

Excited now, the boys got permission to skip the rest of their classes, which were just parties anyway. They spent the day completing step number 14,182 of the checklist -- bolt the plexiglass viewport in place.

As soon as school was out that afternoon, the entire student body and the Danfords gathered around the entrance to the garage. Several of Mike's friends from the band played an impromptu fanfare that sounded something like a flock of sick seagulls. Then, to a lot of cheering, the door to the shop opened and the submarine was rolled out on its dolly.

Someone had called the newspapers and television stations and they were there in force, taking pictures and interviewing Mike. That night there wouldn't be a person in the county who didn't know about the Great Submarine Project, as the press dubbed it.

The hand shakes and congratulations went on for an hour, along with promises of rides once the sub was proven seaworthy. As the crowd began breaking up, Mike heard another familiar voice.

"Cast off the stern line, maties, we've got a tide to sail!"

Mike swung around. "Admiral Norton! What are you doing here?"

"Did you forget I have spies?" he joked. "They called me this afternoon and said you were planning to have a grand rollout." His face turned to mock disappointment. "When I didn't get a personal invitation, I decided I'd have to crash the party."

Mike was instantly horrified at his own oversight. "Oh Admiral, I'm sorry! I didn't even think . . . I mean I never expected . . . well it was just supposed to be a few . . . ."

Admiral Norton laughed. "Don't worry about it, Mike. You had a lot on your mind. Besides, I really came over to talk to your dad about a test program."

The admiral thoroughly inspected the submarine, shaking his head in wonder. "Mike, Josh, you've really built a beautiful piece of machinery here!" he said. "I think I'm jealous. All I have are those little nuclear things the Navy builds. And they don't even have windows!" Everyone laughed, but knew the admiral was sincerely impressed.

After the inspection, the sub was rolled back into the shop. The admiral, and of course Josh, were dinner guests that night, and the submarine was the only subject discussed.

With the help of Admiral Norton, Mike's father laid out a strict test program for the sub. It started on Monday when Mr. Danford had it trailered to a pipeline company. He had taken a week of vacation from his job as an aerospace engineer to help with the tests.

"What's first on the agenda?" Josh asked, as he and Mike rode along in the front seat of Mr. Danford's pickup.

"We're going to x-ray the sub," Mr. Danford replied.

Josh looked puzzled. "What for? We already know what's inside."

"We're x-raying the welds," Mike's father explained. "The people at the pipeline company are experts, and can detect the slightest flaw in the joints. A flaw which, incidentally, could crush the sub in deep water."

"In other words," Mike added, "we're going to see how good you were with that welding torch!" He watched Josh's face go a little pale.

It took most of the day, during which Josh paced nervously, as did Mike. Finally the procedure was complete, and the "patient" was declared perfectly healthy. Mike shouted and slapped Josh on the back. "I knew I could trust you!" he told his friend.

As they followed the boat back to Seacrest, they got caught in rush hour traffic on the freeway. Cars were backed up for a mile as people slowed to gawk at the submarine.

"I guess from now on we'd better cover it up when we move it," Mr. Danford decided.

They spent Tuesday and Wednesday filling and re-filling the air tanks and working all the valves again and again. Mike left the electronic equipment running day and night to see if it would fail.

Wednesday evening they ran the first pressure test. After closing the hatch, Mike filled the inside of the sub with compressed air, raising the pressure. For two hours the boys sat and waited, watching the inside pressure gauge. If the pressure went down by even a single pound per square inch, it would mean air was leaking out somewhere. The needle didn't even quiver, though, and the test was a success.

Thursday was the day Mike had been waiting for. A crowd gathered as a rented crane lifted the sub off its semi-truck trailer and placed it gently into Admiralty Sound. This time Mike couldn't hold back a few happy tears as he watched his bright yellow craft bobbing gently in the foamy green water. Sunlight sparkled off the shiny hull and crystal clear bubble. Even Josh was moved by the sight, and Mike saw him swallow hard to keep control.

"You really did it, Mike."

"Yes, *we* really did!"

As the boys climbed inside the floating sub for the first time, it was almost as if it had taken on a life of its own. It was just tall enough that the boys could stand upright without hitting their heads. Even though consoles of equipment lined both sides, there was still plenty of room to move, and the portholes placed to either side of the seats made it feel even more spacious. It's not just a hunk of metal sitting in the shop anymore, Mike thought. Now it's a real submarine!

"I'm proud of you son," Mr. Danford said with an arm around his son's shoulder. "You set out a goal for yourself and worked hard to achieve it."

"Thanks, Dad," Mike said with a grin. His father's words made Mike feel warm inside.

"And by the way," Ben Danford added with a sneaky smile. "I've called the Inspector for the American Bureau of Submarines. He'll be here at 9:30 tomorrow morning to supervise the final tests."

"Oh great!" Mike moaned, and the warm feeling of a moment before turned to new stabs of fear.

All that day they ran surface tests, cruising around the cove while checking the motors and electronic gear. The temptation to take the sub on a dive was strong, but Mike resisted. He knew it was not yet certified as safe.

That evening Mike and Josh tied the sub to the marina gas dock, since it was too heavy for the boat elevator. Construction on the new wing of the marina had begun, but was not yet complete. Being summer, there were attendants on duty all night who would keep an eye on the sub, which sat under giant floodlights.

Josh stayed with Mike that night, sleeping on the floor in Mike's room as usual. They talked until late, too excited to sleep.

"What if it sinks tomorrow?" Josh asked.

"Don't *say* that! I don't even want to think about it."

They had just decided it was time for a midnight snack and were going out the bedroom door when a loud crash made them jump. A rock flew through Mike's window, landing right where Josh had been sitting a moment before.

They both raced to the window and looked out, but could see no one. Giving up any hope of catching whoever had thrown the rock, they went to examine it. Wrapped around the rock was a note on plain white paper. Scrawled in red ink was a cryptic message: STOP THE SUBMARINE PROJECT OR DIE!

CHAPTER EIGHT

THE ADVENTURE BEGINS

A pounding on the front door woke the rest of the Danford household. Mike and Josh were there first, followed immediately by Mike's father in shorts and a t-shirt. After looking through the peep hole, Mike opened the door to one of his Navy bodyguards.

"Is everyone all right? We couldn't see what it was that guy threw."

"We're okay," Mike said. "It was just a rock."

"My partner's chasing the guy. I'd better go help him." Before the intelligence man could leave, his half-bald partner ran up, breathing hard.

"He's long gone," he panted. "Had a motorcycle stashed over on the next block."

"He must have sneaked up through the bushes," the first agent said. "We didn't even see him, just heard the breaking glass."

Once again the police came, and once again, after examining the rock, they said there wasn't much to go on. They took the note to check for fingerprints, but there was little hope of finding any.

The two bodyguards promised to watch more carefully, and everyone went back to bed. Mike and Josh moved to the guest room because of the broken window. Both found it difficult to sleep.

"Josh, you awake?" Mike whispered into the dark.

"Yeah."

Mike swallowed hard. "I'm scared, Josh. Someone is out to get me and I don't even know why."

"I'm scared too, Mike. Someone is out to get you and I keep getting in the way!"

Mike laughed. "I guess being my friend is kind of dangerous these days." He became serious again. "I've prayed about it, and in my head I know God will protect me. But I still can't help being scared. It just seems like my prayers are useless."

"I know what you mean," Josh said.

"I'm starting to think the best thing to do is lock the sub up in a warehouse somewhere and leave it."

Josh was silent for a minute, then asked, "Are you serious?"

Mike thought about it. "Yes, I am," he said. "I'm just so tired of being a target. Maybe we can finish the sub next summer, after things cool down."

Josh didn't reply, and eventually fell asleep. Mike didn't sleep at all, though, and just after dawn he slipped on a pair of jeans and a t-shirt. Outside the window was a tree Mike had climbed when he was little. Now he used it to sneak out of the house without the Navy men seeing him.

Seacrest Beach was Mike's favorite place in the world, and that's where he went now to think about all that had happened. The salty morning air did nothing to cheer him this time, though, as he walked along the wet sand.

After half an hour he sat on a big piece of driftwood and gazed toward the marina a quarter mile away. As he stirred the sand with his bare feet, he thought about his submarine, and how hard it was going to be to just lock it up and forget it. He began to feel bitter toward the unknown forces that were threatening him, and kicked out at the sand in helpless anger.

"Mornin', boy." The unexpected voice from behind him startled Mike. He turned and saw an old man with a long beard, wearing a torn raincoat and sagging fisherman's hat. Mike had never seen the man around town before. A bum, he thought, irritated. Just what I need today.

Normally Mike would have been very kind to the man, but his own problem was all he could think of now. "Morning," he said gruffly, and turned back toward the waves.

Without invitation, the man ambled over and sat next to Mike. The old leather rain slicker let off the pungent odor of fish and diesel oil. He stared at Mike for a moment, then said, "So yer gonna quit, huh?"

Mike's head snapped up and he looked with surprise at the stranger. "What do you mean?" he asked suspiciously.

"Yer gonna quit. The submarine. Right?"

Mike stared for a moment, confused. "How did you know?" he said softly.

"Don't take no genius to figure it out." The old man coughed and spat into the sand. "I seen yer picture in the paper, an' I read about them things happnin' to ya. When I seen ya walken the beach with that look on yer face, it jest all fit together."

Mike dropped his gaze to the sand. "So. It's the only smart move. There's no sense taking stupid chances for some stupid submarine ride."

The man pulled out some beef jerky, bit off a piece with his crooked teeth, then offered some to Mike. When Mike declined, the stranger talked as he chewed. "Ya know, it seems to me yer lettin' fear get to ya." He looked crosswise at Mike, one eyebrow raised. "Good Lord said we don't have ta be scared, ya know."

Mike was silent for a moment, then said, "You know the Lord?"

The old man nodded. "All my life," he said. "Never let me down, neither.

Can't say as I haven't let *Him* down a few times, mind ya, but never t'other way 'round."

Taking the stranger more seriously now, Mike looked him square in the eye. "But don't you think there's a point where we have to use our common sense? Don't you think God gave us that sense so we'd know enough not to stick our hands in the middle of a fire, or jump off a cliff?"

"Sure I do," the man said. Then, with a smile, he added, "But thar's a big diff'rence 'tween common sense about things ya know, and just being scared of what ya don't know."

Mike thought this over for a minute. "But it just doesn't seem very smart to take chances for . . . for something that's just a big toy."

The old stranger sighed deeply and sat up straight. "Well, ya gotta decide fer yerself what to do. But just 'cause it seems like a toy now, doesn't mean it'll always be that way." Then he leaned over and said softly into Mike's ear, "Ya never know what the Lord has planned." He stood and pulled his tattered raincoat around him tightly. "All I know," he said, "is I never got nothin' by runnin' scared. An' I got *every*thing trust'en in Him."

After a few moments of silence, Mike turned to say something, but the man was gone. Looking around quickly, he could find no trace of the stranger. He must have crossed the street into the woods, Mike decided.

Mike walked the beach for another half hour. Finally, he made a decision, then quickly walked up the hill to his house. He waved to the startled guards sitting in their car, then ran through the front door and up the stairs to the guest room.

With a playful kick, he woke Josh, then jumped on his own bed. Josh looked at him in surprise. "Where've you been?"

"Oh, I just went for a walk," Mike answered. "Josh," he said cautiously, "do you believe in angels?"

Josh looked at his friend suspiciously. "Well, I suppose so. Why?"

"Oh, nothing," Mike said quickly. "Anyhow, you'd better get your lazy behind out of bed. We've got a submarine to test!"

"You're going ahead with it?" Josh asked in surprise.

"Yup. I decided I can't be scared of the unknown. Take precautions, yes, but be scared, no."

Mike's parents went along with his decision, though Mrs. Danford said she wasn't too thrilled about it. At nine o'clock Josh, Mike and his father went to the marina. A Navy barge was just pulling up to the dock as they arrived. The barge held a giant crane with a large drum of rusty cable.

"Morning, Mike." It was his boss. "What's up for today?"

"Hey, Jordan. Today we find out just how good my sub is. We're going to drop it to fifteen hundred feet and see if it comes back up again. In one, uncrushed piece."

Despite his humor, Mike felt the old pangs of nervousness again as they prepared for the test. At 9:30 exactly a rental car pulled up to the pier and parked. The door opened and out stepped a short little man with thick glasses, and a perfectly trimmed mustache that reminded Mike of his mother's eyelash brush. The man pulled on a grey rubber raincoat, even though there wasn't a cloud in the sky, and put rubber covers over his shoes. With a tattered leather briefcase in one hand and a large book in the other, he waddled down the gangplank like a penguin.

"Danford!" he said, snapping his eyes back and forth among the dozen people on the barge. "Mike Danford!"

Mike raised his hand nervously. "Uh, here, sir."

The man looked Mike up and down as if he were surprised to find him a teenager, but he set down the briefcase and held out his hand. "Roland Clayton," the man said abruptly. "American Bureau of Submarines."

Mike shook Mr. Clayton's hand. "Nice to meet you sir. My submarine is . . ."

Before Mike could say more, the man picked up his briefcase again, pushed past Mike and everyone else, and started climbing into the sub, which was lashed to the side of the barge. Mike and Josh shrugged at each other, then followed. When they had climbed down the ladder, the boys saw that Mr. Clayton was already at the controls, checking every switch, dial and valve.

"Uh, that's the main ballast transfer there . . . ."

The Inspector ignored Mike, obviously having already figured that out himself. Mike and Josh kept quiet for the rest of the hour Mr. Clayton worked. Finally he said, "I'm done here," and all three exited. Once back on the barge he said, "You may proceed with the tests." Mike couldn't tell what the Inspector was thinking, or if he was at all pleased with what he was seeing.

At Mr. Danford's direction a tug maneuvered into place and began pulling the barge and sub out to the middle of the Sound.

"Dad, are you sure we have to drop it all the way to fifteen hundred? What it if gets crushed?"

"That's the whole point. I'd rather have it crush while you're standing here next to me than wait until you're down inside of it. It's going all the way!"

When they reached the deepest part of the Sound, the Navy men hooked a cable to the sub. Mike's father checked the fittings, then gave his approval.

"All right son, jump inside and open the ballast tanks."

"Right, Dad." Mike climbed in the sub and pulled the valves that allowed seawater to enter the two pontoons on its bottom. The crane's cable tightened but held fast as the sub gained weight. When the tanks were full, Mike shut off the valves, exited the sub and sealed the hatch.

As Mike said a quick prayer under his breath, and with Inspector Clayton watching from the shade of the crane, the workmen slowly lowered the sub into the dark green waters. Yard after yard of cable was played out, and with each turn of the drum Mike became more nervous. If the sub didn't hold up he'd be out thousands of dollars and hundreds of hours of work.

The minutes passed as the cable meter showed five hundred feet, six hundred, seven hundred. Mike and Josh watched intently for any air bubbles, a sign that the sub was leaking. Half an hour had gone by and the sub was at twelve hundred feet. Mike could hardly stand the tension.

"I feel like I'm about to be a father," he joked.

"I know what you mean," his father said in complete seriousness next to him. Mike looked at his father, and for the first time in his life began to understand why parents are sometimes afraid for their kids.

Finally the meter showed fifteen hundred feet and Mike relaxed a little.

"Now we wait," his father announced. "We'll leave it there for two hours."

Time seemed to stand still for the boys. They ate the lunch Mrs. Danford had packed, talked to the seamen, and laid in the sun. Inspector Clayton sat on a tool box filling out form after form, and Mike wondered how many things he'd found wrong with the sub. Finally his long, sleepless night caught up with Mike, and soon the gently rocking barge rocked him to sleep.

"Okay, bring her up!" Ben Danford's cry woke Mike with a start. His stomach started to churn again. What shape would his craft be in? Even though he knew it was still hundreds of feet down, Mike couldn't keep himself from leaning over the side of the barge, watching for the sub to appear. When at last he saw its yellow exterior come into view he and Josh began shouting.

"It's okay, it's okay! It didn't collapse!"

When the sub was once again tied up to the barge, Mike opened the hatch. The interior was perfectly dry. That didn't seem to impress Inspector Clayton, however. He scowled as he tapped the hull with a tiny hammer, shaking his head every few seconds. Then he climbed inside again, and it was another agonizing hour while Mike and Josh waited on the barge. Finally Mr. Clayton stuck his head out the hatch and asked Mike to hand him some papers from his briefcase. With surprise Mike saw that the papers were copies of the blueprints for the sub.

The Inspector disappeared down the hatch again, and it was another twenty minutes before he finally climbed out and stood next to Mike on the barge. Shaking his head slowly from side to side he said, "Young man, I'm very sorry, but your submarine design has one fatal flaw."

Mike's heart sank and his voice was shaking as he said, "Oh. What's that?"

Mr. Clayton cleared his throat, scowled even harder, and said, "The flaw is that I didn't think up this design myself!" Then the Inspector broke into a huge grin and shook Mike's hand. "Congratulations, son," he said. "You have designed and built a simply marvelous machine!"

It took Mike a second to realize what was happening, then he finally let out a whoop and slapped Josh on the back. "We did it!" he yelled, and the two jumped and hollered like they'd just won the state football championship again.

"Congratulations, son," Mr. Danford said with a slap on his son's back. "Your sub is hereby officially approved by both the American Bureau of Submarines *and* the Danford Testing Agency!"

Dinner that night was a celebration. Both of Mike's sisters were there as well as Admiral Norton, Mr. Stevenson, Inspector Clayton, the two Navy guards, Jessica, and many of Mike's friends. Everyone had a good time and the party lasted late into the night. Of course, the main item on the menu was submarine sandwiches.

The next morning, Mike and Josh were out of bed early and began preparing for the first self-contained dive. Down at the dock they hooked a compressed air hose to the outside fitting on the sub to fill the tanks. They connected another fitting to a battery charger on shore.

By ten o'clock a large crowd had gathered. People stood on the piers, along the road, and down at the beach. The news agencies were there again, and were setting up for a live broadcast of the event during the noon news.

Mike's family arrived, along with Jessica, Jake, Mr. Johnson, Mike's boss and many other friends. Finally the moment came for the first voyage. Mike had already decided that Admiral Norton and Mr. Stevenson should be the first two passengers.

The night before, Mike and Josh had carefully completed the last step on their checklist by painting the secret name of the sub on its hull. Once the paint was dry, they had covered it with a piece of canvas. As he stood next to it now, Mike prepared to uncover the name. With television microphones shoved in front of his face, Mike nervously made a short speech.

After giving recognition to Mr. Stevenson, Admiral Norton, and the others that had helped, Mike concluded.

"But above all, this project was completed by the grace of God, and it's to Him that I give the most credit. He's protected me in every situation, and I have faith He always will. So in naming the sub, I chose a name that represents not only the sea, but symbolizes the absolute necessity of faith in God."

With that he ripped off the canvas covering the name. "I hereby christen this submarine, The Jonah!"

The crowd burst into thunderous applause, and Mike, Josh, Admiral Norton and Mr. Stevenson climbed aboard. Inside, the sub was a mass of technology. Digital displays covered the walls and ceiling. Chrome-plated valve levers and gleaming pressure gauges sparkled in the sunlight streaming through the windows.

The four freshly upholstered seats sat in a row, each movable forward and backward on a special track. Mike took the front seat, which faced directly out the five-foot window created by the bubble. He slipped in behind the converted airliner steering wheel and ran his hands over the controls. To the left of the steering column was the throttle. This lever would make the electric motors run faster or slower. To the right of the column was a brass compass and depth gauge. And centered on a pedestal in front of the steering column was a flat-screen computer monitor that had graphic images of the most important gauges. Here Mike could see his compass heading, depth, speed, pressure in the ballast tanks, and so on.

Behind Mike sat Josh. On Josh's right were the banks of valves that controlled the flow of air and ballast throughout the sub. Over his head were rows of gauges showing the air pressure in each tank and the power level in each battery. He also would control the air-regeneration system from his position.

Directly behind Josh was the periscope, and behind that Admiral Norton's seat. In the fourth seat at the back of the sub was Mr. Stevenson.

Each crew member had a good view out the front, as well as a porthole on each side. A scuba tank was strapped to the back of each seat.

Admiral Norton was the last to enter the sub, closing the hatch behind him. "All set, skipper."

Mike reddened at the admiral's kindness in calling him a name reserved for boat captains. "Thanks, Admiral," he said. Then to the whole group added, "If you'll all please listen for a moment, I'll explain a few of the safety features. You'll notice that you each have a scuba tank on the back of your seat. Please notice where the regulator is hooked to the wall on your right."

After they had each done this, Mike continued. "These tanks are for emergency breathing. The sub has an air monitoring system. It constantly sniffs the air looking for poisonous gas. If it finds any, it sounds this alarm." Mike pushed a button sending a high-pitched sound through the sub.

"It's highly unlikely that we'll ever have a problem of poison gas, but if it should happen in this small space it would only take seconds before you'd be overcome. So if you ever hear that alarm, don't ask any questions. Just grab your mouthpiece and start breathing from the Scuba tank."

Mike explained a few of the sub's other features, then it was time to go. He signaled the dock hands to cast off, then eased the throttles forward and guided the sub out into the bay.

The gently rolling waves washed over the front bubble as the sun sparkled off its clear plastic surface. The bottom half of the bubble was already underwater, and the mysteries of the deep seemed to call to the submariners. Unable to wait any longer, Mike started reading the pre-dive checklist.

"Seatbelts," Mike called from the form.

Josh looked around. "Check."

"Air bottles."

"One through eight full at twenty-two fifty pounds."

"Batteries."

"Ninety-eight percent."

"Air supply A."

"Charged."

"Air supply B."

"Charged."

"Electronics bay."

"Master switch on."

They went through the entire list that way, Mike reading off each item, Josh checking it. Admiral Norton folded his arms and smiled at their thorough, professional manner.

"Hatch."

"Closed and sealed."

"Pressure check."

Josh opened the valve that let compressed air into the sub. When the pressure gauge showed the sub to be airtight he reported, "Pressure in the boat."

"Checklist complete." Mike grinned widely. "Well, this is it. Flood negative!"

Josh opened the valves that let water into the ballast tanks and the sub began to descend. They watched the green foaming water slip up and over the clear front window, and in a moment they were submerged. They dove to fifty feet and Mike tested all the controls.

Moving the control column forward caused the sub to point downward. Pulling it back made them go up. Turning the steering wheel to the right or left put the sub into a perfectly smooth bank and turn in that direction.

After getting familiar with how the sub handled, they dove to the bottom, some hundred feet down.

"It's *beautiful*," Mike yelled.

White sand and colorful sea plants covered the bottom of the Sound. Fish of every size and shape cruised slowly around piles of rocks where starfish and crabs shared their homes. Occasionally the bottom would erupt in a cloud of sand as a flatfish came out of hiding and swam away.

The group talked excitedly about the sub's performance. "I've been in dozens of subs," Admiral Norton said, "most of which I've designed. But I've never had *this* much fun! I've never been in one with a window before!"

Mr. Stevenson was equally impressed. "That first day you came to me, I had my doubts, Mike. But you guys have actually done it!"

For half an hour they cruised slowly past colorful sea life, chasing fish and dodging seaweed. Finally, it was time to return. "Blow ballast," Mike ordered, and Josh sent air to the tanks, pushing out the seawater.

They popped to the surface a hundred feet off the dock and the crowd cheered. Reporters surrounded the group as they climbed out of the sub.

"I am very impressed," Admiral Norton told them. "These young men have done a magnificent job in designing and building this submarine."

Mike's mother and father were the next to take a ride, and Laura Danford especially loved it. "It's as thrilling as the time I went skydiving with the King of Norway!" she said as they passed through three hundred feet.

Next were Mike's two sisters, and Katie had a thousand questions. "How come you have a depth gauge if the computer already shows your depth?" she asked.

"It's a backup, in case the computer crashes."

"Smart thinking," Katie answered. "And what's that funny readout on the computer screen with all the arrows and squiggly lines?"

"That's our GPS," Mike answered. "Global Positioning System. It tells us exactly where we are on the earth by taking readings from satellites out in space."

All day long Mike and Josh took friends down in the sub, stopping occasionally to recharge the batteries and air. Even a television reporter and cameraman took a ride.

Jessica also enjoyed the underwater cruise. When they returned to the dock Mike blushed as she gave him a kiss on the cheek in front of everyone.

The last dive of the day came just before dark. Mike and Josh were exhausted, but they didn't mind a bit. Two of their friends climbed down the ladder and Mike went through his safety speech for the umpteenth time that day.

The sun was low on the horizon and the water dark as they dove to the bottom of the bay. Mike switched on the outside lights and they revealed an entirely different world from that of the daylight.

Darting in and out of the beams of light were colorful fish that hid during the day. Other night creatures emerged from the rocks, and the boys looked out in awe.

Revived by the fresh scenery, Mike decided to take the sub out farther and deeper to areas they had not yet been. Swinging the sub around, he followed the sandy bottom out toward the middle of the Sound.

As they passed over a large pile of crusty rocks, an enormous octopus suddenly jetted past them through the light. Scared by the strange intruder, the octopus left behind a cloud of inky liquid as a smoke screen.

The depth gauge was edging toward two hundred feet and Mike decided they had gone far enough. Pulling back on the throttles, he slowed the sub and then let it gently touch down on the bottom. They sat there, in eerie silence, waiting to see what creatures would pass before them.

For the hundredth time Josh checked the gauges over his position. They showed the batteries at fifty-two percent and the air tanks at twelve hundred pounds, about half full.

After a few minutes, Mike started the motors again and a cloud of sand enveloped the sub. As he guided the boat in a smooth left turn, the scream of the Master Alarm pierced the air.

Shocked, Mike looked at the alarm panel overhead. The flashing red screen gave a frightening message: POISON GAS IN THE BOAT!

CHAPTER NINE
A DEEP DIVE

Without waiting, Mike grabbed his scuba mask and pulled it over his mouth and nose. Turning around, he saw the others had done the same. Behind their masks his two friends had wide eyes and white faces.

"Don't panic," Mike's muffled voice came through the mask. "We're safe as long as we breath from the tanks."

Pushing the throttles full forward, Mike pulled back on the wheel as Josh emptied the ballast tanks. For a moment it seemed as if the sub wouldn't rise, but finally it responded to the controls and headed topside. They rose quickly then, and all were relieved when they at last broke through the surface.

Still at full power, Mike guided the sub toward the gas dock. The churning propellers left a wake of white water. Seeing this, and hearing the screaming motors, the crowd sensed that something was wrong. When the sub approached the dock there was no lack of hands ready to help.

Before they exited the sub, Mike took a canteen they had brought along, emptied the water out into the bottom of the boat, and waved it around in the air. Capping it securely, he answered Josh's questioning gaze. "It's so we can find out what kind of gas leaked."

Each taking one last deep breath from the scuba tanks, the four boys climbed out of the sub and into the cool night air. Once on the dock, they finally relaxed. The two passengers were shaking, having obviously been very frightened.

The next day Mike had the canteen of gas analyzed but was puzzled by the report. "It shows perfectly normal air," he told Josh. "I don't get it."

With nothing else to try, Mike removed the air testing unit from the sub and checked it out on his workbench.

"Here's the problem," he said at last. "We have a burned-out microchip. I must have used too much heat when I soldered it." As he replaced the part, another thought struck him. "This means there really wasn't any poison gas. We weren't in any danger at all!"

"I'm just as glad we took the precautions," Josh said. "I'd rather breath scuba air than poison air."

Over the next several days, Mike and Josh spent every possible moment in the submarine. They discovered that its top speed was fifteen knots on the surface and five knots underwater.

"What's a 'knot?'" Mike's sister Amy asked.

"Nautical Mile Per Hour," Josh answered. "It's a little longer than a regular mile."

"Why not just say 'Miles Per Hour' like everyone else?" she asked.

Josh gave her a teasing look like she was really dumb. "Because we're on a *boat* and boat-type people use '*knots*.'"

Amy said she didn't understand, and Josh said that was okay because he didn't really either.

The boys also discovered that the sub could dive from the surface to 100 feet in 45 seconds, and that they could safely stay underwater for eight hours, if they were careful about using the batteries. Both of them learned how to guide the sub smoothly through the water, banking and gliding like a porpoise.

New sights greeted the boys on every trip. Strange looking fish, rock formations, even old cars and sunken boats filled the viewport. Mike's curiosity led them to explore every part of Admiralty Sound.

One afternoon Mike was just getting off work when Josh showed up for their daily dive. Josh was carrying two large pizza boxes and a cooler of pop.

"What's all this?" Mike asked.

"A vital necessity for every future voyage. Our lunch."

"Lunch! Is food the only thing you ever think of?"

"Not the only thing, but close to it. Besides, yesterday you kept me down there for six hours with no food. My stomach can't handle that!"

Mike shook his head and laughed. "All right rover, bring your stomach and let's get going."

The boys climbed aboard the sub, which was still tied up at the gas dock. Work on the marina was progressing rapidly, but it would be at least three weeks before the sub's new home was ready.

After completing the checklist the boys headed out of the harbor and dove to fifteen feet.

"How come so shallow?" Josh asked.

"I thought it was about time we learned to use the periscope. Trade me places."

Josh moved into the front seat and Mike took the second, moving it back behind the periscope. He unfolded the handles and pulled up on the scope, causing it to rise above the waves overhead.

"This is fantastic!" Mike spun the scope around, watching boats go by. As he watched, he popped a Jolly Rancher in his mouth and said, "Since we're so shallow, you'd better listen on the sonar, in case a boat comes in from a direction I'm not looking."

Several minutes passed as the two cruised around the entrance to the harbor, trading places several times. It was during one of Josh's turns that the plans for the day changed.

Still looking through the scope, Josh spoke half to himself. "Well, well, look at this."

"Look at what?" was Mike's reply.

"Something I think you'll find very interesting."

"Girls?"

"No. Doctor BakerBoyd cruising out of the harbor in his boat."

Mike made a quick decision. "What's your bearing?"

"Zero-nine-four degrees."

"Down scope."

"What?"

"Down scope!"

"Why? What are you . . . "

"Josh, just put it down, will you?"

Josh did as his friend asked. "Okay, but will you tell me what you're up to?"

Mike wasn't listening. He had the hydrophones over his ears. With his right hand he turned the knob that rotated the microphone on the outside of the hull. "Got him!"

By now Josh was exasperated. "Got *who*? What are you doing?"

"BakerBoyd. I've got his engine on sonar. We'll follow him with this so there's no chance of him seeing the periscope.

"Oh no, not again," Josh moaned. "I thought you gave up on spying."

"We're *not* spying. We're just looking. I just want to see what that stuff on the bottom of his boat is."

"It's none of your business, that's what it is. Mike, there's nothing wrong with   doing . . ."

"I know, I know," Mike interrupted. "But this is different. This *feels* right!"

"You've said that before," Josh mumbled as he shook his head. The boys followed Dr. Boyd's boat for fifteen minutes, until it slowed to a crawl in the middle of the sound. Mike pulled back on the throttles and hovered two hundred feet behind the cabin cruiser.

"Okay, now we find out. Trade me places again."

As they moved, Josh couldn't help commenting. "I hope you know what you're doing. It would sure be embarrassing to get caught in his fishing lines."

Mike was at the periscope now, carefully raising it until he made sure Boyd was not looking their direction.

"Okay I-spy, what do you see?" Josh was obviously not happy about the whole thing.

"He's letting out some fishing line . . . it's coming straight back toward us."

Even as Mike said it, Josh could see the flash of a metal spinner approaching, carried by the current.

"Here it comes," he called. "Uh, Mike, take a look at this."

Mike lowered the scope and went forward next to his friend. Outside the front window the fishing line was only three feet away. Instead of the usual lure on the end there was only a lead weight with no hook.

"What do you make of it?" Even Josh was getting curious now.

"I don't know, but he sure doesn't plan to catch many fish. Why don't you back us out of here so we don't get tangled in it?"

As Josh moved the sub to the left, Mike went back to the periscope. "He's in the cabin," Mike said, "talking into a microphone."

"Why would he come clear out here to talk on a radio?"

"Don't know. Wait a minute . . . he's not talking on the regular radio. I can see the marine radio over by the steering wheel."

"So what's he talking on?"

"Hard to say. All I can tell is that it's definitely a microphone. Let's try something else. Take us down and move over under the boat."

Josh looked at his friend in disbelief. "*Under* the boat?"

"Yeah, this *is* a submarine you know."

"Okay, but I'm not sure I'm that good at handling this thing yet."

"I have faith in you," Mike replied.

Despite his self-doubt, Josh controlled the craft expertly. Soon they were ten feet under the boat, pointed slightly up, looking at the strange "Christmas tree" protruding from its bottom.

"I don't believe it," Josh said, seeing the bottom of the boat for the first time. "It *does* look like a Christmas tree."

"What'd I tell you? But we still don't know what it's for. I wish we could get a look inside that hatch."

As if by Mike's request, the hatch suddenly opened and a steel sphere started to snake out on the end of a cable. It had only unreeled a few yards when suddenly it stopped, then reversed direction and was quickly pulled back inside the boat.

"What was that all about?" Josh asked.

"I don't know, but let's go back up and see what's going on up there."

Josh maneuvered the sub back out from under the boat and rose to periscope depth. Mike once again looked through the scope.

"He's talking on the microphone again and looking around like he lost something in the water . . . wait a minute . . . he's looking in our direction . . . he's got a pair of binoculars . . . he's looking right at us!"

Mike slammed the periscope down. At the same moment they heard the roar of the boat engine, even without the sonar. In the next second the boys saw the bow of the boat cutting through the water coming straight at them.

Without hesitation, Josh shoved the throttles forward while Mike pulled the lever to fill the ballast tanks with water. The boat roared overhead, missing the sub's conning tower by inches.

At a safe depth now, the boys relaxed.

"That was close," Josh said.

"*Too* close. How did he know we were here? It's like he knew right where to look."

"Maybe that sphere was a sonar microphone," Josh offered.

"Maybe . . . but it was already inside the boat when BakerBoyd spotted us."

"Well, however he did it, he did it. Now we're in for it."

"No we're not. All he saw was the periscope. He doesn't know who it was."

"Mike, even I'm smart enough to figure out there's only one submarine within five hundred miles."

"Yeah, but it's not like he's going to go back to the marina and call my dad."

Josh gave Mike a disgusted look. "So you're going to try and keep it from your dad?"

"No, you're right," Mike sighed. "I guess we'd better talk to him when we get back."

"That should be interesting."

The boys cruised for another hour, not wanting to meet the Doctor back at the marina. Finally, they headed back to the dock. There was no sign of Boyd, and they went straight to Mike's house and told his father the story. Admiral Norton was also there, having come to talk to Mr. Danford.

"Mike, I don't believe it!" Mr. Danford was quite upset. "I thought we agreed there would be no more spying on Doctor Boyd."

"Yes sir, we did. I just couldn't help being curious about that boat. It looks so strange."

"Mike," Admiral Norton interrupted, "what you've described goes along with what I came over to tell your father. Our investigators checked up on Doctor Boyd. It seems he's doing some independent research on the movements of killer whales . . . kind of a hobby. The gear you've told us about sounds like just the sort of equipment one would use in such research. The sphere probably *was* an underwater microphone, used for listening for the whales."

"But who would he have been talking to?" Josh asked.

"Not who, but what," the admiral answered. "One of his experiments is to try to attract the whales using different sounds, including the human voice."

After a few minutes of talking, Josh and the admiral left. On the way out, Josh shot Mike a look that said, "I wish I could help you." Mike could only shrug and wave goodbye.

When they'd gone, Mike sat uncomfortably under his father's stare. "I guess my curiosity got the best of me," he said before his father could speak.

"Well, to make sure you have time to get it under control," Mr. Danford said, "you're restricted from the sub for a week."

"But *Dad!*" Mike wanted to argue but his father's stare made him think better of it. "Yes sir," he replied.

Later, talking to Josh on the phone, he vented his frustrations. "I can't stand it anymore! No one seems to care that there's someone out to get me. Even *you* think I'm nuts."

"Not true," Josh said. "I support you one hundred percent. It's just that I don't think BakerBoyd has anything to do with it."

"He must! Why else . . . oh never mind." Mike decided it was useless to argue.

"Mike, we've been best friends for ten years," Josh said. "If you really think BakerBoyd is part of this, I'll back you up all the way. But will you please just consider the possibility that it might be someone else?"

Mike let out a sigh. "Yeah, I guess you're right, Josh. If I only look at one possibility I might walk right past the real guy and not even know it. Thanks for sticking with me."

Though Mike missed the daily trips in his sub, the week was not a total loss. He spent every day with Jessica, walking along the beach, or at the park, or window shopping in the nearby cities.

When finally the week came to an end, the boys took the sub out for a dive to get back in practice. The next day Josh met Mike at the marina just as he was getting off work. Mike had recharged the sub's batteries and air tanks earlier in the day, so they left the harbor immediately and headed to the middle of the sound.

"Where to today?" Josh asked. He was already munching on a piece of pizza.

"I thought we'd try for a depth record. We're going straight out to the middle and dive to a thousand feet."

Josh almost choked on his pepperoni. "You mean like twice as deep as five hundred feet?"

"Yup."

"I think I forgot to do my homework. We'd better go home."

"This is summer. There's no school."

"I like to get an early start."

"Relax, Josh. We both know this thing can dive to fifteen hundred."

"I know it *can*, I just never thought we *would!*"

In answer, Mike called for Josh to flood negative. Josh reluctantly opened the valves that sent water to the ballast tanks and the sub slipped below the waves. They dove slowly, passing schools of herring and sea bass. As they glided past six hundred feet there was almost no light filtering down from above and Mike switched on the two forward headlights.

"What's *that!*" Mike screamed, pointing out the front window. A huge brown fish was poking its nose at the sub.

"It's just a basking shark," Josh answered.

"What do you mean *just?* That thing's as big as a semi truck!"

"Don't exaggerate, Mike. It's no more than thirty feet long. And harmless since they only eat plankton."

"How can anything that big be harmless? Maybe you were right. Maybe this dive wasn't such a good idea."

As if he heard the boys talking, the shark slammed the side of the hull with his powerful tail, leaving them shaken but otherwise unharmed. Mike was as white as the sand at Seacrest Beach. "If that's harmless, I'd hate to see your idea of dangerous."

"He's just playing," Josh answered. "We're safe inside the sub. Even a shark *that* big can't break two-inch steel." Then with a punch to Mike's shoulder he said, "Hey, this dive may not be so bad after all. I might get to see some more deep-water sea life!"

"My friend the biologist," Mike groaned. "What have I done?" While Mike enjoyed math and science, Josh was more interested in animals. He hoped to be a veterinarian or biologist some day.

The shark followed them for a while, then, bored with its new toy, swam away into the darkness. The sub was now at nine hundred feet and still descending.

"Okay, Josh. Start blowing the ballast so we can level off at a thousand."

"Coming right up, oh skipperly one." Josh pulled the air valve open and waited for the hiss and gurgle that normally accompanied ballast operations. There was only silence. He pulled the lever again, but still nothing happened.

"Uh, Mike," he said nervously, "I can't seem to blow the ballast."

"Check your routing valves." Mike was so sure of his sub that the thought of a malfunction never entered his mind.

"They're all set right. Main supply routed to ballast system B, to ballast control panel. But it doesn't work!" Panic was now starting to creep into Josh's voice.

Mike was just annoyed. "Here, let me try." He checked the valves and worked the levers but still the craft sank lower. "It must be stuck," he concluded.

"Mike, look at the depth gauge. We're passing a thousand feet!"

Now even Mike was becoming concerned. "We're okay for a while," he said, trying to reassure himself as much as Josh. "We can go to fifteen hundred with no problem."

"I hate to be a party pooper, Mike, but look at the depth finder."

Mike gasped as the reality of the situation hit him. They were plummeting out of control, and the depth finder showed the water to be more than two thousand feet deep!

CHAPTER TEN

A SHOCKING DISCOVERY

"Twelve hundred feet!" Josh screamed. "We're going all the way!"

The tiny sub was gaining speed as it plunged toward the bottom. Mike and Josh frantically worked the levers that should have filled the ballast tanks with air.

"Try the main cutoff!" Mike yelled. "Maybe we forgot to open it."

Josh quickly tore up one of the deck plates and reached below. "It's wide open." A second later he cried, "Mike! We're passing thirteen hundred!"

Nothing Mike did made any difference. His mind raced as he went over the possibilities, but everything pointed to one conclusion: they were going all the way to the bottom. "God help us!" he whispered a prayer.

Mike pulled back hard on the control stick and then shoved the throttles all the way forward. This should have sent the sub shooting to the surface, but with the weight of the full ballast tanks all it did was point the nose up as the sub plummeted downward.

The deeper the sub plunged, the faster it went. Mike saw the speedometer peg out, then riveted his eyes to the depth gauge. He watched as the numbers flashed wildly on the display, almost too fast to read. As they approached the crush depth of the sub, Mike called out, "Fourteen hundred!"

"Only a hundred feet to crush depth," Josh yelled. "Six hundred to the bottom!"

The roar of the water rushing past thundered in Mike's ears. The motors shrieked at full power. Alarms screamed warnings.

"Fifteen hundred!" Mike cried. His whole body began to shake with fear as he waited for the sub to crush like a pop can under a giant foot. At any moment, tons of water would crush and drown them. "Jesus help us!" he wailed, tears streaming down his cheeks. "Please don't let us die!"

The sub raced past sixteen, seventeen, eighteen hundred feet. Just past nineteen hundred an explosion shook the craft and it began shaking violently. Mike fought with the controls but nothing he did helped.

I don't want to die! Mike kept thinking. Please God, I don't want to die!

Mike no longer saw any of the instruments. He stared straight ahead at the water rushing past, expecting the Plexiglass windshield to shatter before his eyes.

Both boys screamed as another loud bang and bone-jarring crash threw Mike to the floor. He saw Josh smash head-first into a panel of gauges. The sub spun wildly, spiraling downward at a steep angle.

In one second Mike saw a flash of white as the sub struck the sandy bottom. The next second was an explosion of lights and sounds. Darkness and silence followed as Mike blacked out.

At first Mike couldn't figure out where he was. A moment ago he had been lying on the warm Seacrest Beach talking to Jessica. Now everything was cold and dark and painful. Suddenly he snapped fully awake as he realized what had happened.

His first thought was for Josh. The overhead lights were out, but in the dim red glow of the instruments he saw blood running down the side of his friend's unconscious face.

"Josh!" Terrified at the thought that his friend might never wake up, Mike pulled himself up the tilted deck to help Josh. Please Lord, don't let him be dead! Mike thought.

Reaching for Josh's wrist, Mike soon found a strong pulse. He tore off his t-shirt and pressed it against the gash on the side of Josh's head.

"Josh, can you hear me?"

A groan from his friend brought relief to Mike. "Come on, buddy, wake up."

Josh's eyes fluttered open, and with some effort he was able to speak. "Mike? What are you doing here? You're supposed to be working . . . "

"Just lean back and relax, Josh. We've had a little accident."

Now Josh snapped awake as he realized where they were. He looked around the sub, scanning the various instruments. "Mike! The depth gauge!"

Mike spun his head to the front of the sub. The computer had been knocked out, but mechanical backup gauge still functioned. It showed the sub at a depth of two thousand eighty-three feet! They were sitting right side up on the bottom, with the nose of the sub pointed downward.

"I don't believe it," Mike whispered as he stared at the gauge. Grabbing a flashlight off the bulkhead he shined it around the interior of the submarine. He then lifted the floor plates and checked the bilge. "Well, I don't know why," he said, "but we're not leaking." Then turning back to Josh, "How's your head?"

Josh closed his eyes and leaned back against the periscope. "It feels like a busted watermelon," he answered. The bleeding was slowing down and Josh continued to hold the cloth to his head. "And I think I ruined your favorite t-shirt."

Mike smiled for the first time. "If that's the worst that comes out of this, I'll be happy."

With his friend taken care of, Mike turned his attention to the lights. He discovered that the circuit breakers had all popped, and soon had them back on. Just having the lights back on raised Mike's spirits. But he noted that the computer screen remained blank, and was thankful they had built in mechanical backups for all the most important systems. Looking out a porthole, he saw that the sub was resting at the base of a cliff.

"What now, oh skipperly one?" Josh was starting to get back to normal.

"First thing is to send up the buoy." Mike reached overhead and turned a lever. A distant thud confirmed that the door had popped open, releasing the buoy that would guide a rescue team. A radio at the marina was always tuned to pick up the automatic distress signal.

"Now we'll take care of you."

"I'm okay," Josh said, "just a little bump on the head."

"Right. That's why my white t-shirt is now red." Mike broke out the first-aid kit and put a large bandage on Josh's head. As he worked, he began thinking about the situation they were in. He could feel panic rising in his chest again, and forced himself to relax and think straight. I've got to get Josh out of this mess, he thought.

With the dressing applied, Mike sat back in silence. Finally Josh spoke what was on both their minds.

"You think we're gonna die, Mike?"

Mike thought for a moment. "I don't know, Josh. We've got about six hours of air left, and plenty of battery. But it's going to take time for them to get down to us. And they probably won't be expecting us to be this deep." He paused for a moment, then looked his friend straight in the eye. "I guess if we're gonna get out of this, God will have to help."

For the next several hours the two friends sat quietly, straining to hear the sounds of rescue ships. They tried the sonar, but the microphone on the outside of the hull had been destroyed in the crash. All they could do was sit and wait.

A while later Mike turned to his friend. "Josh," he said solemnly, "we have another problem."

Josh's face tightened with dread. "What now?" he asked softly.

Mike took a deep breath, held it for a few seconds, stared his friend in the eye, and said, "I'm out of Jolly Ranchers."

The two boys collapsed in laughter. "You jerk!" Josh laughed. "You really scared me!"

"Sorry," Mike answered, wiping tears off his cheeks. They fell into another spasm of laughter, and for a while they forgot about the seriousness of their situation.

It wasn't long, though, before Mike began thinking about his parents again. They seemed so far away. They're only a mile from here, he thought, but they might as well be in Australia. He also missed his sisters and Jessica terribly.

Five hours after sinking, Mike made a decision. He grabbed the toolbox and, after turning off the air supply, started taking apart the bank of air valves. "If I'm going to die," he explained to Josh, "I'm at least going to find out why!"

With Josh's help, he soon had the valves apart, but they were in perfect condition. "I guess we'll never know," Mike said.

"Hey, what's this 'never' stuff. You giving up already?"

Mike gave his friend a long look. "Truthfully, Josh? I don't think there's going to be a rescue. We're just too deep. And we don't even know if the buoy really worked."

Josh leaned back against the bulkhead. "I'm scared, Mike," he said softly. "I keep thinking of all the things I haven't done yet, and all the people I love. I don't want to die."

Mike took a deep breath. "I guess it's times like this when you find out how much God really means to you."

The next hour passed slowly for the boys. They took turns praying, but eventually ran out of things to say. Several times they thought they heard boat engines overhead, but none of them seemed to be stopping over their position.

The air was becoming thick, and it was getting hard to breathe. Mike watched the air pressure gauges hit zero. He then opened each of the scuba tank valves in turn until they were also empty. As the last tank finished spilling its air, Mike swallowed hard. "We only have the oxygen left inside the sub now," he whispered. The air recycling system was still running but that could only remove carbon dioxide. It had no more oxygen to add.

Forty minutes later Mike lay on the floor gasping for air. He moved next to Josh and put his arm around his friend's shoulders. "Josh . . . thanks . . . for being my . . . friend."

Tears ran down Josh's cheeks. "Thank you . . . Mike. I'll see you . . . in heaven . . . ."

As the air continued to thin, both boys began seeing strange flashes of light and hearing odd sounds. They were becoming disoriented as their oxygen-starved brains began failing.

Suddenly there was a loud hiss and a blinding light. Mike and Josh felt a rush of cool air hit their bodies. The sweet smell of oxygen filled their lungs and they sucked in deep breaths. Their minds started to clear and they looked up. Centered in the open hatch above was the face of Admiral Norton.

The admiral scrambled down the ladder carrying a tank. He immediately put oxygen masks over Mike's and Josh's mouths and noses. "Breathe deep, boys," he said. "You're all right now."

Neither of the submariners could understand what was going on, but they didn't care. The oxygen was all they needed to know.

Captain Washington was right behind the admiral and began checking the boys over. In a few minutes they still felt weak, but otherwise normal. Mike was the first to remove his oxygen mask.

"Admiral Norton . . . how did you get here?"

He smiled a big smile. "By a little thing called a DSRV . . . Deep Sea Rescue Vehicle. We have one based at Keyport in case one of our subs goes down. It's a kind of little submarine designed to reach a sunken sub and attach to its escape hatch. Since you bought your hatch from us, it mated perfectly."

Both boys were sitting up now, and Josh asked the next question.

"Can we go home now?"

The admiral laughed. "You bet. There are a bunch of worried people waiting up there. When they picked up the distress signal they sent out a boat of divers, but they discovered how deep the water was so they called us." Then he looked around the sub and said, "By the way, why isn't this thing as flat as a pancake?"

Mike and Josh looked at each other, smiled, and looked back at the Admiral. "God!" they answered together.

The four climbed aboard the DSRV, which was like the inside of a big pop can with benches along each side. After closing the hatch and attaching a line to the Jonah, they began the long ascent to the surface. The trip up took almost an hour, during which Captain Washington gave the boys a thorough examination.

When finally the rescue vessel surfaced, Mike and Josh opened the hatch and basked in the sunshine. A navy boat sped them to the marina dock. When Mike saw his parents and Josh's mom standing there waiting, he knew for sure that he was all right. Hugs, kisses, and tears flowed as the boys told the story of what had happened.

"I don't know what could have gone wrong," Mike said to his father. "The valves were working perfectly but no air would go into the ballast tanks."

Several hours later the Navy solved the mystery. Admiral Norton's men had raised the sub and then inspected it. He was at the Danford house now, reporting his findings.

"It was sabotage."

Mike felt like a steel wall had slammed into him at the admiral's words.

"Someone, who knew a lot about submarines, put a small valve in the air system where it enters the ballast tanks," the admiral explained. "It was set to prevent air from entering the tanks once the sub had passed a hundred feet. That way the system would work during the pre-dive checkout, but not later. Mike and Josh were doomed the moment they passed a hundred feet."

The group sat for a moment thinking about what the admiral had said. Mr. Danford was the first to break the silence.

"Do you have any idea why, Buck . . . or more importantly who?"

"No, we don't. Mike, do you have any ideas?"

Mike stood and walked to the window, his anger just under the surface. "Yes, I do," he said finally. "But you won't like it. All my problems started the first day I got a look at the bottom of Doctor Boyd's boat!"

"Now Mike, let's not start that again."

"But Dad, think about it . . . "

"I have thought about it, Mike, a lot. There's just no reason to suspect Doctor Boyd."

"Then *who*?" Mike felt exasperated. He wanted to yell out, "Why won't you believe me?" but he held his temper in check.

"I don't know, Mike," his father answered. "I guess we'll have to let the admiral and the police solve that one."

That was the end of the conversation, but the question of who could have sabotaged the sub haunted Mike all night. He prayed for a long time, and then suddenly realized that God had been with him all along. Even with all the close calls, he thought, I haven't been seriously hurt! After that, he was able to fall into a deep, sound sleep.

The next morning Mike and his parents had a long talk.

"Just to be safe," his father said, "I never want you to go where the water is more than a thousand feet deep. Also, I want you to make a thorough check of all the sub's systems before you leave the dock."

"I'd already planned that," Mike replied. Then looking at his parents he said, "I know the Lord saved us yesterday, but I don't want him to have to work overtime."

There were no further developments over the next two days, which Mike spent repairing the sub. He discovered that the motor pods had been crushed, which was probably the explosion they'd heard. With Josh's help, he quickly made new ones.

Mike filed another police report, and the police were sympathetic, but there were still no suspects. Admiral Norton's men also came up empty.

"We even checked out Doctor Boyd, Mike, just to be sure. He barely left the hospital for the twenty-four hours prior to the sub sinking. Since you used the sub the day before, we know it was working then. It had to have been tampered with that night, and Doctor Boyd was in surgery."

"Thanks, Admiral," Mike sighed. "I guess we're stumped again."

"Maybe so, but we still have men watching you, and I put a few watching the sub as well. Whoever is behind this won't get near you, or the Jonah, again."

That night Mike had a date with Jessica, and he was looking forward to seeing her. He picked her up at her house and was taking her to dinner at a seafood restaurant. As he pulled away from the curb, he noticed a brown sedan following them.

"Well, there they are again," he said.

"There who are?" Jessica asked.

"My bodyguards. They drive a different car every day, but I can usually spot them after a while."

"Well, it's nice to know you're being protected."

"Yeah, I suppose." He turned and looked at her. "But sometimes I wish I could lose them for a while."

Mike enjoyed the dinner of steak and crab with baked potato, but more than that he enjoyed Jessica's company. Afterward they sat and talked for a long time while sharing chocolate mud pie.

"So what does a junior in high school do for excitement after he's built a submarine, been chased by crooks, and spent a few hours on the bottom of the ocean?"

Mike's face flushed at the attention. "Oh, I thought tomorrow I'd climb inside a volcano and ride a lava flow."

"I wouldn't put it past you!" she laughed. A moment later she spoke again. "Seriously, Mike, promise me you'll be careful."

"I *have* been careful. It's just that someone is very determined to get me."

After paying the server, Mike helped Jessica on with her coat and escorted her to the car. As he held the door open for her, he looked up and saw a familiar face approaching.

"Hey Nick! Haven't seen you in a while. How ya doing?"

Nick Travis smiled broadly as he saw his friend. "Great, Mike, how about you?"

"Great. Jessica and I just had dinner at the Cliffhanger. Where're you headed?"

"Down to Seacrest. I'm meeting a friend at Salty's in an hour."

"That's a long walk. You want a ride?"

Nick looked from Mike to Jessica and back. "Uh, that's okay. I can hoof it."

"No, really Nick, it's no trouble. Jessica doesn't mind, do you Jess?"

"Of course not."

"Great!" Mike said. "Hop in, Nick." Mike pulled away from the curb and began the drive to Seacrest. "I haven't seen you for a while, Nick, what've you been up to?"

"Uh, I've been working for my uncle . . . up in Sun View. I'm making big bucks, too. How about you? Been taking your sub out a lot?"

"Just about every day. We've, uh, had a few problems, but I think we've got them worked out now."

"What do you do down there, anyhow? Look for sunken treasure?"

Mike laughed. "No, just kind of cruise around to see what's there."

"Have you found anything interesting?"

"Oh, not really. We found a couple cars that were dumped out there, and a couple boats that sank. But mostly we just see fish and rocks." A few minutes later he said, "Well, here you are, Nick. Salty's Diner. Hope you don't have to wait too long." Then with a grin, "Is this friend a girl or a guy?"

"Just a guy, unfortunately. But I can have my pick of girls up in Sun View any time I want. Well, I'll see you later. Bye Jessica."

Mike and Jessica spent the rest of the evening watching the waves from the marina and talking. After he took her home, Mike couldn't stop thinking about her. He had never felt like this before and couldn't figure out what was going on. One thing he did know, however. He wanted to see a lot more of Jessica Kingston!

It was two weeks later that Admiral Norton once again came to visit the Danfords. Over a dinner of turkey and dressing the admiral made an announcement.

"I'm afraid I have some bad news. My superiors have ordered me to remove the surveillance on Mike and the submarine."

Ben Danford looked disappointed. "Well, I knew it had to happen sooner or later. I just wish we could have found out who's behind this first. Mike, how do you feel about it."

"Both good and bad, I guess. It made me feel good to know they were there, but it will be nice to take Jessica on a date without them watching."

"Maybe I'd better watch," Mike's mother joked.

"I tried to forestall this," the admiral said, "but it's been a month since the last incident, so the official Navy view is that there's no justification for continuing. Also, they need all the security men we've got for our own submarines. We're almost ready to launch the Nebraska and security must be tight."

"Don't worry, Admiral," Josh broke in. "I'll take care of Mike."

"I think I'm really in trouble now," Mike groaned.

They talked through the rest of dinner, and it was late that night before the admiral left.

"I won't be seeing you for a while," he said, "I have to go to Washington D.C. But if you need anything, just call my aide, Commander Ramsey, and he'll take care of you."

"Oh yeah," Mike said. "We met him when we were there the first time."

"That's right. Well, I'll be off. Take care of yourself, Mike."

"I will. Thank you, sir."

Mike was a little nervous knowing he was on his own again. To make up for it, Mike's parents talked to Josh's mother, and Josh accepted the Danford's invitation to move in with Mike for the rest of the summer. They even moved a second bed into Mike's room so Josh wouldn't have to sleep on the floor.

Two days later the new addition to the marina was finished and the boys sailed the sub into its new home. Mike was obviously pleased with the setup.

"This is fantastic! No one can get near the Jonah now."

One part of the bottom floor of the addition could slide open on tracks. A cement ramp extended from there down into the water. All Mike had to do was maneuver the sub under the building to the ramp, where it would mate with a special dolly. A winch then pulled the sub up into the building, keeping it dry and safe. Jordan had even thought to have a circle of shower heads installed to rinse off the salt water as the sub was pulled up the ramp.

"I don't know how to thank you, Jordan. This is just great."

"Oh, I can think of one way you can thank me," he said with a smile. "The entire first floor needs to be painted with wood preservative."

Mike grinned. "No problem. Josh will help me."

Josh started to object but decided against it. "Sure, why not."

That afternoon the boys once again went cruising in the sub. They had been down for about an hour when Mike heard a strange sound on the sonar.

"Josh, listen to this."

Josh was eating his third piece of pizza, but took time out to listen.

"Hey, that sounds like a pod of killer whales!"

"Yeah. Let's follow them!"

Josh frowned. "Won't work," he said. "They're just like any other animal. They'll run as soon as they hear our motors."

Mike thought for a moment, then checked a tide table and chart. "We don't need the motors. The tide's going out and the current will carry us to them."

"So what are we waiting for?"

Mike took the sub down to the bottom and cut the motors. Without power, the sub started to drop, but Josh's expert use of the ballast controls kept them level.

The boys drifted with the current for more than an hour, the sounds of the whales growing louder every minute. Steering the sub was not easy without power, but Mike managed to guide them in the direction of pod. As they got closer, he became a little nervous.

"Maybe this isn't such a good idea. What if they don't *like* submarines?"

"Relax, they're friendly," Josh said.

"Then why are they called 'killer'?"

"That's just a name. Quiet now, we're almost there."

Mike already had the outside lights on, and they both now strained to catch a glimpse of the whales through the Plexiglass. They were drifting just above the bottom at three hundred feet, moving at about five knots.

Suddenly Mike saw a slow moving shadow just beyond the edge of the light.

"There they are!" he yelled, pointing.

"Where?" Josh asked

"Right *there*."

The shadow was closer now. Suddenly a wave of shock flashed through Mike. "Josh," he gasped, "that's no whale. That's a submarine!"

CHAPTER ELEVEN
A DANGEROUS FRIEND

Outside the plastic bubble the dark shadow moved slowly past. The murky water made identification difficult, even though the massive size of the object filled the viewport.

"See," Mike shouted, "there's the conning tower."

"I see it," Josh said. "I think."

"What do you mean, you *think*? It's right *there*! Look, there's some writing on the side." Mike pointed to a dim white outline on the monster. A second later it was gone from view.

"Well, whatever it was," Josh said, "it's gone now."

"That's what *you* think." Grabbing the throttles Mike shoved them full forward and steered in the direction the shadow had taken.

"*Wait!*" Josh yelled, but it was too late. "Now you spooked them. We'll never catch up."

"You can't spook a submarine, Josh."

Josh started to speak but was interrupted by a violent shaking of the craft. "What was *that*?" he yelled.

"Backwash from that submarine's propellers."

"Or from the tails of a dozen giant whales."

"How could you mistake that for a whale? It was a solid wall!"

"Sorry, Mike, I just couldn't see that well. My view from the second seat isn't as good as yours, you know. If you say it was a sub, it was a sub. But what's it doing here?"

"I don't know, but I'm sure going to report it."

"Uh, are you sure you want to do that?"

"I have to."

"Okay, okay. But let's just say it *might* have been a sub."

Mike gave his friend a look of disgust. "I'm telling you Josh, there's no doubt about it." Suddenly something else occurred to him. "Hey, listen. The whale noises have stopped."

"That's what I said. They were scared away when you started the motors . . . uh . . . I mean when that *other* sub started *its* motors."

"They couldn't get away that fast. We should still be able to hear them."

"Wrong, Mr. Biology. Animals are *my* area, remember. They're just like people. When they get scared they stop talking."

"All right, but I still say it was a sub."

They searched the area for another twenty minutes but found nothing except sand and rocks. Since their batteries and air were almost half gone, they decided to head back to the marina. As soon as they had secured the sub in its new berth, they went straight to Mike's house.

Dialing the number for Keyport Naval Base, Mike soon had Commander Ramsey on the phone. Mike remembered the commander as being tall and muscular, with square shoulders to match his square jaw.

"Well Mike, good to hear from you. Admiral Norton told me you might call. Did you find the whales you were chasing?"

Mike almost dropped the phone. "Uh, yes . . . I mean no . . . I mean . . . how did *you* know?"

The commander laughed. "Did you forget we have a very expensive set of underwater ears over here?"

"Yes, I guess I did. You mean you could hear us down there?"

"Of course. We've tracked you every time you've gone out since your accident. Today we heard you head in the direction of the whales then cut your motor. We figured you were trying to catch them. Then we picked you up again right in the middle of the pod when you started your motors. *That* sure spooked them!"

"Yeah, I guess it did. So you heard the whales huh?"

"Sure. They're out there all the time. That particular pod has been there for a couple months now."

"Well, that's what I was calling about, Commander. I got a good look at one of them, and it didn't look like a whale to me."

"Oh, is that so. What did it look like?"

Mike hesitated for a moment, doubt beginning to creep into his mind. "Well, it sort of looked like . . . a submarine." He held his breath, waiting for a reaction from Commander Ramsey.

There was silence on the other end of the phone for a moment. When the commander spoke, his skepticism was obvious. "Did you say a submarine, Mike?"

"Yes sir. A very big submarine. Just like you have over there."

There was another moment of silence. "Well, Mike, we have the only subs in this part of the world, except for yours of course, and we've had none in that section of the sound for months. I'm afraid you were mistaken."

Mike felt like he had been kicked in the stomach. "Commander, sir, I *know* what a submarine looks like, and this *was* a *submarine*!"

"Let me explain something to you Mike," the commander said patiently.

"Everything that moves under the water makes at least a little bit of noise. Submarines, no matter how quiet they are, make a *lot* of noise. That's how we're able to track you. There's no sub in the world that could get into Admiralty Sound without our hearing it. Besides, we both heard the pod of killer whales. The chances of both the whales *and* a submarine being in the same place just as you happen upon them are millions to one."

Mike leaned against the wall, his body sagging in disappointment. "Yes sir, I guess you're right. It just looked so much like a sub."

"Vision gets distorted underwater, as I'm sure you know. The water bends the light rays and plays tricks on your eyes. Did your friend see the same thing you did?"

Mike had been dreading this question. "Uh, well, not exactly. He was sitting farther back and couldn't see as well. He's not sure what he saw."

"Well Mike, I thank you for your concern and for calling this to my attention. Most people would have ignored it. You did the right thing in calling. But I can assure you that if a submarine gets within a hundred miles of our shores, we'll be aware of it."

"Thank you, Commander. I'm sorry I bothered you."

"No bother at all. I appreciate your calling. Goodbye."

"Bye, Commander."

Mike hung up the phone and looked over at Josh, who was slouched on the sofa. "Don't say a word," Mike warned.

"I wasn't going to say anything," Josh said with a look of hurt. "Except maybe that I should drive next time we go submarining."

The pillow Mike threw caught Josh square in the face. "The last thing I need is you saying 'I told you so,'" Mike said with a laugh.

"But it's true, I did."

Mike threw another pillow, and the two friends were into a wrestling match.

"Hey you two, watch out for the furniture." Mrs. Danford was just coming into the house carrying two bags of groceries. Mike jumped up to help her in. "What have you boys been up to today?"

Mike looked at Josh and they made a silent pact. "Oh, nothing much. Just a routine dive in the sub."

Summer was half over by now, and several of Mike's and Josh's friends from school invited them to a beach party one night. The parents of one of their friends were holding the party at their beach house a few miles from Seacrest. Mike, Jessica, Josh, and Josh's date Cindy arrived about seven and the party was already going. A bonfire of driftwood was burning in the middle of the beach, with pots of crabs and clams boiling away.

"Oh man, smell that food!" Josh exclaimed, sniffing the air.

Mike couldn't pass up an opportunity to tease Josh about his appetite. He grabbed Josh and yelled to the girls, "I'll hold him back while you make sure everyone else gets to eat first."

The girls laughed as Josh escaped Mike's grasp and pulled away. "Can I help it if I have an overactive hunger gland?" he said defensively.

"Overactive! You could eat a good-sized hole in the Western Hemisphere!" Mike said.

The joking continued throughout the night. Despite Josh's huge helpings of seafood, there was plenty for all of the more than one hundred teens. A volleyball game started on the beach under the light of a dozen tropical torches, and the four friends joined in.

Mike and Josh knew most of the people at the party, and traded stories about summer activities. Mike tried to play down the incidents where he had been in danger, but everyone had heard about the sinking of the sub from the news reports, and Mike and Josh were constantly being questioned.

"Do you know yet why the sub sank?" one boy asked.

Josh started to answer but Mike jabbed him in the ribs and interrupted. "It was a malfunction in the ballast system." Later Mike explained to Josh that he didn't want a lot of publicity about the sabotage. Josh agreed this was a good idea.

As usual, there were many requests for rides on the sub, and Mike said that he'd give as many as possible. Nick Travis spoke up in mock disappointment. "You promised *me* a ride and I'm still waiting."

"Oh, Nick!" Mike exclaimed. "I'm sorry, I completely forgot. How about next Monday? I've got the day off."

Nick broke into a wide grin. "That'd be great!"

The party lasted until well after midnight when the host's father finally announced it was time to leave. The boys drove Jessica and Cindy home, then headed home themselves. Mike was deep in thought when Josh punched him in the arm. "Are you in there, Mike?"

"Sorry. I was just thinking about Jessica." He paused for a moment. "Josh, I think I'm in love."

Josh moaned. "Oh no. Now I not only have to protect you but I've got to put up with your love-sickness too."

"If this is a sickness," Mike said smiling, "it's the nicest disease *I've* ever had!"

The boys slept late the next morning, waking up just before noon.

"What's the plan for the day?" Josh asked as he got dressed.

"Have you forgotten already? We're painting the marina."

Josh stopped short and sat down. "Oh, my stomach," he groaned. "I must have eaten a rotten clam last night. I guess I won't be able to help you today."

"Gee, that's too bad, Josh. I guess Jessica, Cindy and I will have to do the painting ourselves."

"Cindy? She'll be there?"

"Yeah. She and Jessica offered to help out. We'll have a blast. Too bad you won't be with us."

Josh sat up straight and rubbed his stomach. "You know, I'm feeling much better all of a sudden."

"I thought you might," was Mike's reply.

The painting party lasted all afternoon and went smoothly, except for the time that Josh knocked over a bucket of the wood preservative. The four artists had half the first floor painted in record time. Mike's sub was the only boat on that floor as yet, so there were no boats to get in the way. The smell of new lumber and fresh paint filled the room.

Mike was high on a ladder painting the ceiling when he decided to stop and rest. Painting overhead was backbreaking work, and his arms felt like lead weights. He sat on the top step, then noticed his sub sitting twenty feet below. Even from this angle the sub was impressive, and he sat admiring it. Suddenly an idea struck him and he climbed down the ladder.

"Hey, what's this?" Josh called. "I didn't hear the whistle blow."

"I just thought of something I want to check out," Mike called back. "I think we're gonna make an addition to the sub."

"What kind of addition? It's already got all the conveniences of home."

"Wait a minute while I look underneath. It may not even work."

"*What* may not work?"

Mike didn't answer, and instead crawled under the front of the sub. After several minutes, he emerged with a grin.

"I think it'll work."

"I give up," Josh sighed. "Just tell me how to build it and then I'll guess what it is."

"No need to wait, I'll tell you now. We're going to add a manipulator arm to the sub."

"You mean one of those mechanical things with a hand at the end?" Mike nodded in answer, and Josh looked doubtful. "Those things cost thousands of dollars just for a normal laboratory. I hate to think what an underwater model costs."

Mike was still grinning. "I figure about twenty-five bucks."

The doubt on Josh's face turned to pure skepticism. "Right. We'll just go down to the local Small Submarine Remote Underwater Manipulator Arm Discount Store and pick one up."

"Not quite," Mike replied. "We're going to build it." Taking a piece of paper, Mike sketched his idea for Josh. When he was finished, Josh sat back and nodded.

"You know, that might just work."

"I hope so. I'll use the computer tonight and log in to Admiral Norton's engineering program. That will tell us for sure."

As Mike finished this last sentence, everything went black. The two boys found themselves clawing at something rough and smelly. When they finally fought their way out of the canvas painter's tarp, they saw Jessica and Cindy standing back laughing.

"What's the big idea?" Josh said.

Jessica was laughing as she answered. "We were just punishing you for goofing off."

Mike and Josh looked at each other, grabbed the tarp and in one swift motion had the girls neatly wrapped up.

"We give up!" Jessica called. "We'll be good!"

They let the girls out, then all fell on the tarp laughing. Finally they composed themselves and sat talking. After a while, Mike made an offer the others couldn't refuse.

"We're almost done painting, so why don't we get busy and finish it? Then I'll treat us all to pizza." The others agreed and within an hour the job was finished.

Later that night Mike was working at the computer when Josh got back from taking Cindy home.

"Well, Einstein, have you figured it out yet?"

"Sure have," Mike replied. Then pointing to the computer screen, he explained his design. "We'll weld a three-inch diameter pipe that's about ten feet long to the bottom of the sub. It will stick out the front of the sub about seven feet, with the back end of the pipe capped so it's watertight. At the front end we'll attach a claw that can grip and rotate."

Josh nodded. "Neat. How do we make the hand do these great things?"

"The two halves of the claw will open by means of a cable pulled by a motor. It will be spring loaded so it will close automatically when the motor releases tension on the cable."

"And what about the rotation?"

"My dad has an old motor down in the basement we used to rotate our TV antenna before we got satellite. We'll put that in a water-tight housing and attach the hand to it. Then we'll tie the whole thing to the main computer and plug a joystick into the game port to move the arm."

"Sounds good to me. When do we start?"

Mike thought for a moment. "Probably not till late next week. I have to work the next several days helping move the boats into the new addition. I also promised we'd take Nick on a submarine ride."

Josh looked disgusted. "Why do you pay attention to that jerk? All he does is brag about himself and tell lies. You're the only guy in the whole school that even listens to him."

"He needs a friend, Josh. Maybe if more people treated him better he wouldn't have to try to make himself sound important."

"Maybe so, but I think I'll still be unavailable on Monday."

Mike sighed. "Okay, I'll take him myself. But will you at least help me get the sub launched?"

"Sure," Josh said, looking ashamed now. "And I'll go along, if you really want me to."

"No, that's okay. It'll give me a chance to talk to him alone."

The next few days passed quickly, with Mike working ten hours every day except Sunday. The new annex was opened and boat owners flocked to reserve a spot in the building. Of course everyone entering the marina was instantly attracted to the submarine, housed safely behind an iron fence that rose to the ceiling, and Mike was kept busy answering questions.

Monday afternoon arrived and Mike, with Josh's help, prepared the sub for launch.

"How are you going to control this thing all by yourself?" Josh asked.

"I'll just set everything before we dive, so all I have to do is pull the ballast lever."

Josh frowned. "Sounds risky. Maybe I'd better go along after all."

"We're only going out a half mile or so, and no deeper than a hundred feet. We'll be okay."

"I still don't like it, but I guess you can handle this thing. How long will you be gone?"

"Less than an hour."

"All right, but promise me you'll come back and get me if you decide to stay longer."

"I promise."

At that, Nick walked up wearing a wind breaker and baseball cap. "Hi guys, what's up?"

"Hi, Nick," Mike said. "We just finished getting the sub ready."

"And I was just leaving," Josh said curtly.

Nick was surprised. "Leaving? Aren't you going with us?"

"Uh, no. I have to go feed my cat."

Nick's disappointment was obvious, and it surprised Mike and Josh.

"Well, I guess if you really have to," Nick said. "I was looking forward to going with both you guys, though. I figured I could show you some stuff I learned from the Navy."

Josh couldn't believe what he was hearing. "*You* . . . were in the *Navy*? And I suppose you served on nuclear subs."

"Oh, I wasn't actually *in* the Navy, I just went on a few cruises. One of my uncles is an admiral, and he arranged for me to go on a two-month tour on an attack submarine."

He can't really think we believe him, Mike thought.

Josh just shook his head. "I gotta go," he said. "See you later, Mike." At that, he left, and Mike turned to Nick.

"Well, let's get this thing in the water. I have a feeling it's going to be a long afternoon."

They launched the sub using the electric winch to ease it down the ramp, then climbed inside. Mike went through the checklist, trying to explain everything to Nick.

"The air supply system enters here and is distributed through this panel."

"That's kind of crude," Nick interrupted, "compared to the *big* boats. They have an electromagnetic system about ten times this size."

Mike sucked in his breath, trying to control his temper. "Well, we do the best we can."

Finally, Mike cruised out a few hundred yards then dove to eighty feet. Despite his claims of submarine experience, Nick was obviously impressed. As they descended through the green waters, he gasped at the sight of colorful fish and plant life.

A half-hour passed and Mike announced that it was time to turn and head back to the marina.

"Oh, not yet Mike."

Mike smiled to himself at Nick's eagerness. "Sorry, Nick. I promised Josh we'd be no more than an hour."

"I don't think you understand," Nick said coldly. "That wasn't a request, it was an order."

Mike could no longer contain himself. His anger exploded as he turned to look at Nick. "Just who do you think you . . . " Mike stopped short as his eyes fell on Nick. In his hand, pointed directly at Mike's head, Nick held a chrome-plated revolver!

CHAPTER TWELVE
A SECRET BASE

"We're not going back to the marina," Nick sneered. "We're going to take a little trip down the coast a ways."

Mike couldn't take his eyes off the gun. If he hadn't known better, he would have sworn the barrel was a foot in diameter.

"What do you think you're doing?"

Nick snorted. "I think I'm doing whatever I please, since I am now in control of this submarine. And I think you will do whatever I tell you or else."

Mike sat silently, glaring at his kidnapper.

"Now face forward and turn to a course of one-seven-six degrees. Then kick this baby up to full speed."

A hundred plans to overtake Nick flashed through Mike's mind, all of which he threw out. Realizing he had no choice, he slowly turned back to the controls and did as Nick had instructed.

"Very good," Nick said. "Just stay smart and you'll get out of this alive."

Mike was steaming inside. His helplessness only infuriated him more. "Would you mind telling me what this is all about?"

Nick laughed a sickening laugh. "Sure, I'll tell you. You and your submarine are now prisoners of the Revolutionary Army of Kirov!"

The name sent a chill through Mike's body. A long-time enemy of the United States, the terrorist group from the country of Kirov were known as killers. Mike didn't even try to hide his disgust. "So, you're working for terrorists. I didn't think even you could sink that low."

Nick was instantly furious. "Shut your mouth, Danford! Just remember who's in control here."

Realizing he'd better be careful, Mike decided to keep Nick busy talking, hoping he'd slip up and give Mike an chance to overpower him. "Why, Nick? You had everything going for you, why help a bunch of terrorists?"

Nick only sneered. "Yeah, I had everything all right. No friends, no family. The other kids at school won't even talk to me. And those goody-goody church people, always talking about love and tolerance. But just let Nick Travis show up and all that fancy talk disappeared. And *you*, you were the worst!"

Mike was stunned by the words that hit him from behind. "*Me*! What did I ever do, except try to be your friend?"

"Yeah, right. At least the others were honest about it. But you had to pretend to be my friend. Don't think I don't know what you said behind my back, though."

"Nick, I never said anything . . . "

"*Shut up*! I don't want to hear it. I know what you're like. Mike Danford. Everybody loves him. Always the hero. Always in the news. He's so smart and so kind and such a good little boy. It makes me sick! Even luck is on your side. If a boat had fallen on me it would have killed me, and even then no one would have cared. But not Mike Danford. He lives through it and is a big hero."

A thought suddenly flashed through Mike's mind. "It was *you*! You were the one on the motorcycle."

Another hyena laugh from Nick confirmed Mike's suspicions. "Yeah, it was me."

"And in the car that followed us . . . and in the shop? That was you too?"

"So you finally figured it out. About time, Danford. And don't forget the rock through the window."

"But *why*, Nick?"

Nick was vicious again. "I just wanted to show you what it's like to be scared!"

They had traveled over a mile by now, and Nick gave Mike a new course to head.

"Listen, Nick. I don't know what you heard, but I've never said anything bad about you. In fact, just the other day I told Jessica what a great guy you are. I always thought of you as my friend. Just look at last week, when you were walking to town. Who was it that offered you a ride?"

Nick laughed again. "Yeah, that was quite a set-up."

Mike's mouth dropped open. "What do you mean, a set-up?"

"My commander had that planned out to the last detail. His men followed you to the restaurant then called me to meet you there. They knew you were so soft you'd give me a ride. My assignment was to find out how much you knew. You were so eager to make points with me that you made it easy."

Mike sat silently for a moment, overwhelmed by Nick's confessions. They passed through a school of sea bass and Mike thought how much he wished he could join their peaceful world. "I suppose it was also your assignment to get me to take you out in the sub."

"That's right, and I did it with no problem. My commander will be very pleased with me. I was supposed to get that jerk friend of yours, too, but you're the real prize."

"And now what's going to happen?" Mike was starting to get nervous.

"Don't worry, they promised they won't hurt you. They're just going to ask you some questions and then lock you up for a while, until they carry out their mission."

"And what's their mission?"

"Even if I knew, you don't think I'd tell you, do you?" Nick paused for a moment then gave a new order. "It's time to check our position. Go up to periscope depth, and be sure you don't let the conning tower show above water."

Mike eased the sub up to the proper depth and held it there. Nick moved to the third seat and raised the periscope. Looking through the scope with one eye, and keeping the other on Mike, he scanned the horizon.

As Nick was doing this, a new hope struck Mike. He remembered that the Navy always tracked the sub with the hydrophones. When Mike didn't return, he was sure that Josh would call Commander Ramsey for help.

Nick lowered the scope and turned to Mike. "We're right on course. Dive back to a hundred feet and then cut the throttles."

"Cut the throttles? What for?"

"Just *do it*!"

Mike did as he was told. The realization of what Nick was doing hit him like a punch in the stomach. He knew in an instant that his rescue would not be as swift as he had hoped.

Nick just sat back and smiled. "Now we wait."

As they reached a hundred feet, a strong current took hold of the sub. It began moving them in the opposite direction from what they had been traveling.

"You think you're so smart, Danford. Don't you think we know the Navy has hydrophones? They can track you anywhere. But in order to track you they have to hear you."

By now, Mike was drenched in sweat. He imagined he could actually feel the barrel of the gun pointed at his back. Worse than that, though, was not knowing where they were going or what would happen to him there. What am I doing here? he thought. I'm only seventeen!

They followed the current for forty minutes. Several times Mike tried to reason with Nick, but Nick only got more furious. The tension squeezed his insides like a giant squid. He gripped the steering wheel tightly and clamped his jaw shut to ward off the panic he felt rising inside. A silent prayer was constantly on his lips.

Suddenly Mike noticed a sound coming through the sonar headphones hanging on the wall. He instantly recognized it as a pod a killer whales. If I could just glide into the middle of the pod, he thought, maybe I could spook them. They'd swim away and rock the boat, then I could overpower Nick.

Before he could finish these thoughts, Nick said, "Okay, take her back up to periscope depth and start your motors."

Again Mike blew the ballast, causing the sub to rise. Searching frantically through the forward viewport, he tried to find the nearby whales. Nick just looked through the scope, scanning all around the horizon. "Now, if you don't want to smash into something, follow my directions exactly."

After several minutes of maneuvering, Nick lowered the periscope and gave new directions to Mike. "Slow down as far as you can. In a few seconds you'll see the end of a pipe. Drive straight in the end and follow it."

Mike started to protest, but the murky water suddenly parted and showed a sheer rock wall with a large black hole in front of them, and he had only enough time to steer the sub into it.

"Pretty neat, huh?" Nick said. "It's an old sewer pipe they don't use any more. It's twelve feet in diameter, so you don't have a lot of extra room. But I have confidence you can make it."

Mike was sweating heavily as he followed the pipe, only inches bigger than the sub. After traveling a hundred yards, he could see a yellow glow filtering down through the water.

"All right, surface."

Mike pulled the valves, and the Jonah bobbed up through a hole in the pipe and into a roughly shaped underground cavern the size of a school cafeteria. Standing on a dock around the pipe were three men holding machine guns.

"End of the line, Danford. Out." Nick gestured toward the hatch, then stepped back, forcing Mike to go out first.

As he climbed out the hatch, Mike saw that the cavern was about fifteen feet high, with lights hanging from the ceiling. A ladder scaled the far wall and disappeared into a round hole. One of the men pointed to the ladder and Mike reluctantly climbed up. Nick was right behind him.

The top of the ladder ended in a room with sparkling white walls and plush carpet. Electronic equipment filled the room.

Mike's captors motioned for him to stand in the middle of the floor, and then one of them pushed a button on a console.

A moment later a slim, handsome man dressed in a crisp white suit entered the room. Mike sucked in his breath as he recognized the man: Doctor Everett Boyd.

"Welcome to my humble home, Mr. Danford. I've been waiting for this moment a long time."

Mike's shock passed quickly. "Well, Mr. BakerBoyd. I guess I shouldn't be surprised. I always thought you were behind all this."

Boyd only nodded, then looked around the room. His eyes finally settled on Nick, who was grinning from ear to ear. "I did it, Doctor Boyd. I got Danford and I got the sub, just like you said."

Boyd gave Nick a cold stare. "And what of Mr. Danford's young friend?"

"Oh, uh, he wouldn't come with us."

In one swift motion Boyd crossed the three steps to Nick and slapped him hard across the face. "You stupid fool! When I give an order I expect you to carry it out. All of it!"

Nick look terrified. "B-but Doctor Boyd, there was nothing I could do."

Boyd slapped him again. "Stop your whining, fool. You're of no use to me anymore. Count it fortunate if I let you live!"

As much as Mike enjoyed Nick's predicament, he also felt sorry for him. He kept reminding himself that Boyd was the real enemy, not Nick.

Turning his attention back to Mike, Boyd spoke again. "Now, Mr. Danford, you and I have an appointment." He turned and spoke to the guards in a foreign language, and two of them grabbed Mike by the arms. The men twisted his arms behind him and Mike winced at the pain. They took him down a long hallway lined with doors.

As scared as he was, Mike still made a mental picture of the floor plan. The hallway and surrounding rooms appeared to be freshly carved out of the rock. The few rooms he could identify were storerooms or bunk rooms.

One of the guards opened a door and shoved Mike inside. There was only one wooden chair, bolted to the floor in the middle of the room. They slammed Mike into it, tying his arms and legs with leather straps.

The guards left and Mike was alone in the room for over an hour. It was cold, and after a while he began to shiver. Images of his other close calls flashed through his mind, and he longed to see Josh burst through the door and rescue him. Finally, the door opened, but it wasn't Josh.

"I trust you've had time to realize there is no escape," Doctor Boyd said. "You are totally dependent on me for life."

Mike sat stone-faced and silent. Boyd merely shrugged.

"Very well, have it your way. Make no mistake, though, you will tell me what I want to know before you leave here."

Mike was fuming inside and spoke for only the second time since arriving. "Don't give me that garbage. You have no intention of releasing me, you traitor."

Boyd smiled. "Let me explain something to you, Mr. Danford. I am a doctor, a surgeon. I know every tiny part of the human body. I am perfectly willing to inflict pain upon you in ways no one else has even dreamed. I hope this will not be necessary, but if you refuse to cooperate I will have no choice." Boyd paused for a moment, letting this sink in.

"Incidentally," he continued, "I am not a traitor. While it is true I was educated in the United States and have lived here ever since, I am a full citizen of Kirov and an officer in the Revolutionary Army."

Mike snorted. "A terrorist. That's even worse. The Revolutionary Army of Kirov is just a bunch of criminals. Even the government of Kirov has denounced you!"

"What you think is of no consequence to me. What you *know* is. And now I shall begin the interrogation. Cooperate and I may let you live. First, why have you been following me for so many weeks, and what did you know of me before today?"

Mike thought for a few moments. He wondered how long he could hold out against pain, and decided probably not very long. And since he really didn't know anything at all, he decided he might as well answer the questions.

"I saw the bottom of your boat the day it fell into the Sound. I was curious about those things sticking out the bottom, that's all. Other than that, all I know . . . knew, is that you're a doctor at Valley General."

"You had no suspicions about my . . . purpose here?"

"I figured you were up to something. I just never figured out what."

Boyd smiled. "Very good, Mr. Danford. Keep this up and I might be inclined to show you some mercy. Now, who did you talk to about me?"

Mike decided he'd better keep Admiral Norton out of this. "Only my father and mother."

Boyd spun around and slapped Mike across the mouth. "Wrong! You also told Admiral Norton of the United States Navy! You spoke to him at your house two weeks ago and told him of your suspicions." Boyd was seething. "I was giving you a test and you just failed. Any more deception and you will be severely punished!"

Mike's mouth smarted and he tasted a trickle of blood from his lower lip. Lord, please help me, he thought to himself.

"Next question." Boyd had instantly transformed himself back into the kindly doctor. "What did you see on your dive three days ago?"

Mike knew it was senseless to lie. "I saw something that could have been a whale . . . or a submarine."

"Ah, now we are getting somewhere. You of course told Admiral Norton of your sighting?"

A plan was formulating in Mike's head and he quickly decided to risk another lie. "Yes, I did. And when I showed him the pictures he believed me."

Boyd's face paled. "And what did these photographs show?"

Mike breathed an inward sigh of relief. Taking the offensive he snarled at Boyd. "A Kirovian submarine lying at the bottom of Admiralty Sound!"

Obviously upset by Mike's answer, Boyd moved his face only inches from Mike's and said in a low, throaty whisper, "Danford, if you're lying to me you are going to die a slow, painful death. Now what did Admiral Norton say when you showed him those photographs?"

Mike forced himself to relax and smile. "He said not to worry, that they had known about the sub since the day it entered the Sound and are just waiting for the best time to blow it out of the water!"

Boyd was visibly shaken by Mike's revelation. Without a word he turned and left the room, slamming the door. Mike took a deep breath and let it out slowly, thanking God for His protection.

A few minutes later the door opened again and Nick Travis entered, quickly and quietly closing the door behind him.

"Have you come to gloat," Mike said, "or are you here to finish the job?"

Nick looked worried and spoke quickly. "Listen, Mike, I know you have no reason to trust me but you're going to have to. We don't have much time."

"Much time for what?" Mike asked suspiciously.

"I don't know what you said to Boyd, but he was sure mad when he came out of here. He started yelling in that funny language they speak and everyone started running around."

Mike smiled to himself. His plan had worked. The Kirovians were scared . . . hopefully scared enough to make a mistake.

"I don't know what's going on out there," Nick continued, "but I don't think either one of us is going to live long if we don't get out of here."

Mike still didn't know whether or not to believe Nick. "Why should that bother you, after you tried to kill us by sabotaging the sub?"

Nick looked genuinely surprised. "I didn't do anything to your sub, Mike, honest. I only wanted to scare you a little. I could never kill anyone."

Either Nick was sincere or he was a great actor, Mike decided. "Okay, so what's your plan?"

"First we get you out of these," Nick said, removing the leather straps. "After that, I don't know."

Free of the straps, Mike rubbed his wrists and thought quickly. "How much do you know about this place?"

"Not much. Only that we're under an old house on Lighthouse Hill. You have to take an elevator to get out, and there's a code you have to enter to do that. I don't know the code."

"There is another way out," Mike said. "The way we came in. But first I have something else I want to try. Does Boyd have an office down here?"

"Yeah. It's farther down the hall on the right. I've seen him go in there but I've never been inside."

"Okay, let's go see what we can find."

Opening the door slowly, Mike peeked around the corner. To get to the sub they would have to go back through the electronics room, where Boyd and his men were located. Fortunately the office lay in the other direction.

Slipping out into the hall, with Nick on his heels, Mike quickly moved the fifteen feet to the door Nick pointed out. His heart pounding, Mike reached for the doorknob. It was unlocked! Before anyone had noticed them, Mike and Nick were inside with the door silently closed behind them.

Mike didn't dare turn on the lights, so he waited for his eyes to adjust to the almost total darkness. When he could finally see, he looked around the room. "There it is," he whispered. Moving over to Boyd's desk, Mike hit the space bar on the computer, bringing it to life.

"What are you doing?" Nick asked.

"Getting help, I hope." Mike tried to open a messaging window, but none was installed on the computer. "What kind of guy doesn't message?"

Nick was confused. "Why don't we just call the police?"

"With all that electronic gear out there I'm sure they have all the phone lines tapped. And there's no way a cell phone would work in this cave, even if we had one."

With that, Mike punched keys on the terminal to open the email program. "That's it! We're in," Mike whispered a moment later. Typing madly, he wrote out a quick e-mail: HELP! HAVE BEEN KIDNAPED BY AGENTS OF THE REVOLUTIONARY ARMY OF KIROV. AM BEING HELD IN BASEMENT OF DR. BOYD'S HOME AT . . . " Where are we, Nick?"

Nick thought for a moment. "The Northeast corner of 6th and Western."

THE NORTHEAST CORNER OF 6TH AND WESTERN, Mike typed. Pausing for a moment, Mike debated over his next line, then decided to go ahead. HAVE CONFIRMED PRESENCE OF KIROVIAN SUBMARINE IN ADMIRALTY SOUND.

Not daring to take any longer, Mike signed his name and sent the message to Josh, his dad, and Admiral Norton marked "Urgent." Then he quickly deleted the email and logs, and put the computer back to sleep. With any luck, at least one of them would check their e-mail soon and call the police.

"Okay, Nick, now let's work on getting out of here."

At that moment the door burst open and two guards stood silhouetted against the light. Pointed directly at the boys were two angry-looking machine guns.

CHAPTER THIRTEEN
A TRICK

Everett Boyd moved between the two guards. "So, Mr. Travis has taken to the other side. Very well, you may suffer the same consequences." Boyd stared coldly at Mike. "And just what were you up to in here?"

Mike stood straight, his lips pursed. Boyd looked around the room, his eyes coming to rest on the computer terminal.

"Never mind, Danford. I think I know your plan." Boyd walked over and brought the computer to life, and scanned its logs. "No emails sent in the last six hours," he said to himself. Then to Mike he added, "You're lucky we got here before you could send a warning, Danford, or I'd shoot you just out of spite."

Turning to the two guards he gave clipped commands in Kirovian, then left. The guards grabbed Mike and Nick and pushed them with the barrels of their guns down the hallway. Passing the room Mike had originally been in, they turned the boys down a narrow corridor. They stopped in front of a locked door which one of the guards opened with a key.

The other guard grunted something in Kirovian and shoved the boys into the small, dark room. The door slammed shut behind them and they heard the key turn in the lock.

Mike felt his way over to the door and found the light switch. When he flicked it on, the single bare light bulb revealed Nick sitting on the floor, crying. He looked up at Mike, trembling. "What are we going to do?"

Mike took a quick look around the room. It was a small, bare storeroom that reminded him of a closet Josh had locked him in when they were ten. It had a musty smell, and dust covered the empty shelves and floor. He searched the entire room closely, looking for any possible means of escape, but there was none. The walls were made of cement and there were no vents or windows. The door that had slammed shut behind them was made of steel, and the hinges were on the outside. And Mike was sure he'd heard a large locking bolt slide into place after the guards had shut it.

"I'll tell you what I'm going to do," he said, sitting down. "Something I've learned to do a lot of the last few weeks. I'm going to pray."

"Great," Nick said sarcastically. "That'll do a lot of good."

Mike spoke slowly, choosing his words carefully. "Nick, I'm not the best example of a Christian. I don't read the Bible as much as I should, sometimes

I get bored in church, and I don't always do what God would want me to do. I do try, and I am growing, but I have a long way to go. But there's one thing I've learned lately, that there is a God and He does take care of me. He's proved that too many times for me to give up on Him now. So I'm going to pray. Not because it calms my nerves or because I don't know what else to do, but because God is here and He does listen."

Nick looked like he was about to get bit by a snake. "Mike, they're not fooling around. They are going to *kill* us!"

Suddenly Mike saw what he had to do, what he should have done long ago. "That's very possible Nick. And I'm not saying that I'm not scared or that I don't want to live. But I trust in God and I know for a fact that even if I *do* die, I'm going to heaven." Mike moved closer and put his hand on Nick's shoulder. "Nick, do you know where you're going when you die?"

Nick hung his head and shrugged self-consciously. "I . . . I guess I'm going to heaven. I mean, sure I've done some bad things, but I'm basically an okay guy."

Mike shook his head. "It doesn't work that way Nick. You don't get to heaven by being good. You get to heaven by confessing to God that you're a sinner and asking Him to forgive you, and accepting Jesus Christ as your Savior." Mike paused for a moment. He had never talked to anyone like this and he was a little embarrassed. He felt a peace about it, though, and as he continued it was easier. "Nick, have you ever done that? Have you ever asked Jesus into your heart?"

Nick looked up at Mike, tears running down his cheeks, and shook his head. "No. But if that's what you have, it's what I want."

Mike felt a warm glow inside. "All you have to do is ask, Nick."

With Mike leading him, Nick prayed for forgiveness and salvation. They said "Amen" and Mike put his arm around Nick's shoulders. "Welcome to the Kingdom, Nick.

After that, the boys talked for a long time, waiting for whatever was coming. "There's one thing I want to get straight," Mike said. "Back in the sub you said I was just pretending to be your friend. That's not true. I really do like you Nick, and I've never made fun of you. Five years ago that wouldn't have been true. Five years ago I didn't care about anybody but myself. I didn't even care about God."

Nick looked of surprised, and it prompted Mike to continue. "Sure, I went to church because my parents made me, and it was something to do. But I didn't really care. Then one day we had a special speaker at church and he made Jesus real to me. He made me realize that Jesus is alive and that He loves me and cares about me. So five years ago, when I was twelve, I prayed the prayer that you just prayed, and started a real relationship with God. But," he added a moment later, "I was still like a lot of the other kids. I was still a selfish jerk."

"You mean like me," Nick said, his head hung in embarrassment.

Mike took a deep breath, trying to think of what to say. "Nick," he said finally, "from what I know, you've had some really rotten things happen in your life. Your dad left when you were little, your mom died and you had to live with an uncle . . . I can't even imagine what all that was like for you. So I can't sit here and judge you. But what I know is this: when I was lying and cheating and being selfish, it never made things any better. It only made them worse."

"Yeah, but like you said, you've had a perfect life."

"I didn't say that," Mike answered, "you did. Yeah, I still have both my parents, and they're great parents too. That doesn't mean everything is always so perfect. But if you don't want to listen to me, then listen to Josh."

"Josh? What's he got to do with it," Nick asked.

"Josh's dad died when he was eight," Mike answered. "After that, his mom had to work at two jobs and was hardly ever home. He had every reason to be mad at the world and start hating everyone. But he didn't. In fact," Mike took a deep breath, trying to decide if he should say this next part, then decided to go ahead. "In fact," he said again, "it was five years ago that Josh and I made a pact."

Nick looked at Mike like he was telling a fairy tale. "You mean like a blood-brother thing?" he asked.

Mike laughed. "Yeah, kind of, but without the blood." Turning serious again, Mike continued. "One day about five years ago, when my dad and I were camping, he asked me what kind of person I want to be — an honest person, or a selfish person. I thought about that a lot, and talked with Josh about it. That's when we both decided we were tired of trying to be cool by being bad. We both decided, and made a promise to each other, that we wouldn't lie or cheat or do anything selfish any more."

Mike leaned his head back against the wall and closed his eyes. "I guess I just decided I didn't want to be that kind of person — that kind of jerk – anymore. I saw the other kids being selfish, and lying to their parents, and acting like they were big shots, and so I started acting that way myself. But after a while, I just got sick of the person I was becoming and decided that's not who I want to be."

Nick closed his eyes for a long time, and Mike wondered if he'd fallen asleep. But after a while, and with his eyes still closed, Nick finally said, "Mike, do you think I could join your pact?"

Mike hesitated. "Maybe," he said. "But you realize that would mean you'd be a 'goody goody.'"

Nick opened his eyes and smiled. "Sorry about that," he said, talking about his put-down back in the sub.

"But I'm serious," Mike said. "What my dad taught me was that there are things that are right, and things that are wrong. You have to decide if you're going to be the kind of person who does right, or who does wrong. That's the difference between being a good person or a selfish jerk."

Nick thought about this for a minute, then said, "I guess I'm tired of the selfish jerk."

Mike smiled. "Then I'll talk to Josh about you joining our pact. But either way, you can still use our formula."

"What's that?" Nick asked.

"It's what we use to remind each other when we start doing something dumb and selfish."

"Yeah, so what is it?"

Mike took a deep breath, hoping Josh wouldn't be mad at him for talking about their secret. "All we say is, 'There's nothing wrong with doing right.'"

Several moments passed as Nick thought about this. "'There's nothing wrong with doing right,'" he repeated. Then he looked up with a grin. "I like it!" he said.

They were quiet for a long time, then started talking again. Eventually the topic turned to Nick's involvement with the Kirovians.

"It was right after the boat crash," Nick said. "I was so jealous after seeing you on the news that I just jumped on my motorcycle and started racing around the streets. Then when I saw you down on the waterfront, I decided to give you a scare." Nick sighed. "As it turned out, I got a scare myself, when Josh tackled me."

Mike thought about that night, and how long ago it seemed. With all the things that had happened since then, the bike attack hardly seemed real.

"Anyhow," Nick continued, "after I got away from you, I turned up Elliot Avenue and got flagged down by Doctor Boyd. His men had been following you all day after the boat accident. I guess they were afraid you saw something. He told me he didn't like you either, and there might be some money in it for me."

"Did you know then they were Kirovian terrorists?"

"No, I didn't find out about that 'till a lot later. Boyd hired me to keep an eye on you and find out what you were doing. When you started building that submarine he really got worried and told me to scare you off. When that didn't work, he told me to get you and Josh to take me out in the sub, then bring you here." Nick rubbed his face. "As you saw, he wasn't happy when I didn't get both of you."

Mike frowned. "Did you really think they wouldn't hurt me?"

"Mike, you've got to believe me!" he said desperately. "I had no idea what kind of people they were. I didn't know anything about the sub being sabotaged, and the gun I pointed at you wasn't even loaded. It was just to scare you." Nick sat back frustrated, embarrassed, and humiliated. "Boyd was always such a nice guy. I thought he really cared about me. He said they were just here to monitor our radio and TV stations." He looked over at Mike. "I guess it must be a little more serious than that, huh?"

Mike nodded. "I think we can safely say they're interested in more than our soap operas." Another thought struck Mike. "You know, Nick, you're going to have to tell the police about this. You're the only one who can testify against Boyd."

"Yeah, I've been thinking about that. Do you think I'll go to jail?"

Mike thought for a moment. "I don't know," he said. "It's possible. But no matter what, the best thing to do is tell the truth."

"I suppose so," Nick sighed. "But it won't be easy."

Mike wondered to himself if Nick was sincere about changing, or if it was just a trick. He decided it would be safest to assume Nick was lying, until his actions proved otherwise.

Time seemed to drag, and Mike became more nervous each minute. I hate just sitting here waiting, he thought. I'd rather face them and take my chances.

A moment later he got his wish. Mike's heart jumped as he heard a key turn in the door and the bolt slide back. Were they coming to check on them? Question them? Or take them to their deaths.

The door opened slowly. One of the guards stood in the doorway holding a gun, while another held a video camera. They recorded the boys for thirty seconds, then left. A moment later Mike jumped up and stepped quietly to the door, listening.

"What is it, Mike?" Nick's urgent whisper went unanswered for a few seconds. Finally Mike turned to him, almost afraid to speak.

"The door," he whispered. "They didn't lock the deadbolt!"

Mike held his breath as he slowly turned the knob. He didn't know if it was a trick or not, but he decided anything was better than sitting around waiting to be killed.

Turning the knob silently, Mike eased the door open a fraction of an inch at a time. A thousand thoughts flooded his mind as he spent long moments scanning the hallway. He could see no movement, and nothing to indicate the guards were nearby.

"What is it?" Nick hissed. "What do you see?"

Mike answered by silently opening the door and stepping out into the hallway. Hugging the wall, he motioned for Nick to follow.

There were three other doors in the corridor and Mike carefully tried each in turn. The first two were locked, but the third one opened. Moving cautiously, Mike tiptoed into the room and waited for his eyes to adjust to the darkness. When he could see that the room was unoccupied, he waved Nick inside and shut the door. Only then did he turn on the lights.

"Do you know where we are?" he asked Nick.

"No, I've never been here before."

Mike surveyed the room. It looked like some kind of sound studio. Racks of digital recorders lined the walls, and a large sound mixing console sat in the middle of the room. "I wonder what all this is for?"

"Beats me," Nick replied.

Mike was curious and wanted to listen to a tape but didn't dare take the time. Instead, he pulled a CD from one of the machines and shoved it under his t-shirt. "That should prove interesting later."

Next he turned his attention to the matter of escaping. The room was small and square and had only the one door. The ceiling was covered with special sound-absorbing tiles, and Mike wondered what was above these. Standing on a chair he lifted a tile and grinned.

"This is a false ceiling. There's enough room up here to crawl through, and it looks like it goes over most the rooms on this floor."

"Let's go," Nick said quietly. "No sense staying around here."

The two boys climbed into the space, closed it behind them, and began stealthily moving from one beam to another. Cobwebs tickled Mike's face, but he kept moving in what he thought was the general direction of the control room. It was hot in the small space, and sweat began to stream off his forehead.

Mike saw light coming up from a vent a few beams away and carefully moved toward it. Stopping when they were directly over the vent, the two boys saw Boyd and his men madly packing papers and equipment into boxes. Boyd was shouting instructions in Kirovian and it was obvious they were getting ready to abandon the tunnels.

Boyd went to a phone on a console and quickly dialed a number. A moment later he spoke calmly in English. "This is Elmer Baker. I was wondering if you could possibly have my boat launched. I'd like to go out this evening and I'm running a bit late." There was a short pause as he listened. "Thank you very much, I really appreciate it." He chuckled at something said on the other end of the phone. "Of course. The combination is forty-two right, sixteen left, twenty-five right." Another short pause and, "Thank you. Goodbye."

Boyd once again yelled out orders, his voice full of hate and anger. Then he nodded to the guard who had put Mike and Nick in the storeroom. The guard grinned widely and pulled back the bolt on his machine gun. He turned on his heel and left the room.

A moment later he returned, pale and jabbering quickly in Kirovian. Boyd slapped the man across the face and began yelling. Mike didn't know a word of Kirovian, but there was no doubt they had discovered the boys' escape.

"I think we got out of there just in time," Nick whispered.

Mike nodded. "We're not out yet, though," he said. "Where do we go from here?" Then answering his own question he said, "This way." Mike started moving again until he thought he was directly above the ladder to the submarine cavern. The complex below was in chaos as Boyd and his men searched the entire place for the boys.

"We've got to get to the sub," Mike whispered. "It's our only chance to get away."

They waited for a few minutes and finally the room below was silent. Mike prayed that all the guards had gone to search and that the room was vacant. Slowly, he lifted the ceiling panel. The ladder was below and about five feet to the left. Close enough, Mike thought. He slipped his head through the opening and scanned the room below. It was empty.

"Now!" Mike said quietly. In seconds both boys were through the hole and had dropped onto the floor below. They took the two strides to the hatch and then froze. Someone was coming up the ladder!

Quickly, Mike gestured Nick behind some filing cabinets. The bald head of a Kirovian guard poked through the hatch. Mike held his breath as the man emerged from the hatch and passed by, two feet from where Mike was crouched.

An instant later, Mike and Nick were through the hatch and down the ladder. Mike couldn't believe what he saw. There was no one else in the cavern and his submarine floated right where he had left it. For the first time in hours, he thought he might actually get away.

"Let's go!" he said to Nick, and they sprinted the few yards to the submarine. Before they reached it, a shout from overhead told them they had been discovered. Glancing back, Mike saw the head of one of the guards sticking through the hatch above.

Without stopping, the two boys sprang to the submarine hatch and in a second had it open. Mike went in first and in one swift motion was down the ladder and pulled the lever to flood the ballast tanks. Nick was right behind him, closing the hatch as he half- fell down the ladder.

Through the front bubble Mike could see the Kirovian guards rushing down the ladder, their loaded machine guns slung from their shoulders. As water flooded over the top of the sub, Mike saw bursts of fire from the guns. Bullets riddled the steel hull, but the resistance of the water slowed them and they bounced harmlessly off the sub.

As soon as they reached the bottom of the abandoned sewer pipe, Mike shoved the throttles into full reverse and they sped backwards down the tube. At that speed, control of the craft was critical. A minor error could slice the hull of the sub like a knife. Mike wanted to get out of there fast, though, before Boyd could do anything to stop them.

Several times the rudders and dive planes scraped the sides of the pipe, and twice the conning tower slammed into the concrete with a sickening "thud." Finally, the water around them began to take on a dim glow and Mike knew they were almost free. In the next second they shot out the end of the pipe and into open water. Mike turned the control wheel to the left to turn the sub around, pushed the throttles to thrust the sub forward, then set the controls to dive deep. When they passed into a hundred feet of open water, Mike finally collapsed in his seat.

Breathing hard, his heart pumping furiously, Mike looked back at Nick. "You . . . okay?" he croaked.

Nick was also trying to recover from the experience. "Yeah. I'm just . . . a little . . . out of breath."

Fifteen minutes later they were back to normal. Already it seemed like their ordeal had been just a nightmare, but both were painfully aware that it had been real.

"Now what?" Nick asked.

"Now we get home fast. My parents are probably going nuts, and I want to get to the marina before Boyd does."

The trip back was agonizingly slow. Mike surfaced once to use the radio, but discovered that the antenna had been sheared off back in the pipe. When finally Nick sighted the marina through the periscope, Mike surfaced and sailed up to the dock.

Night was fast approaching, but the remaining daylight was enough for Mike to see his parents, Josh, and a police officer waiting on the pier. Running down the gangplank, they reached the gas dock just as Mike did. Ben Danford gave his son a hug, and Laura Danford wouldn't let go of him.

"Boyd's coming to take his boat out," Mike gasped. "We've got to stop him!"

Josh shook his head. "Too late. He left an hour ago."

"We've been gone all day, son," Mr. Danford explained. "We didn't check our e-mail until just a few minutes ago. By then he was already gone."

The police officer then entered the conversation. "We have men on the way to the address you gave. We should round up the rest of them shortly."

Half an hour later they were sitting in the marina office, Mike telling his story. Nick told the part about the kidnaping, confessing to having worked with the Kirovians. "Before you say anything more," the police officer said, "I need to tell you that you're under arrest. You have the right to remain silent . . ."

"I know my rights," Nick said. "I don't want a lawyer and I don't want to remain silent. I did what I did and I'll pay the price for it. I just don't want Boyd to get away with anything more!"

"Will the fact that he's the only reason I escaped help Nick?" Mike asked.

"I'm sure it will," the officer said. "But he still kidnapped you at gunpoint, and that's a very serious charge. It will be up to a judge to decide just how serious."

Mike continued his story, but when he got to the part about the sewer pipe, the officer looked doubtful.

"You drove your submarine up a sewer pipe and into an underground cavern?"

"I know is sounds crazy, officer, but that's exactly what happened." Mike didn't blame the officer for questioning his story. Now that he was home, it sounded far-fetched even to him.

Before they had finished, the officer received a call on his cell phone. After a short conversation he hung up and looked at Mike. "Our men went to the house you told us about. It's Boyd's house, all right, but we didn't find anything unusual. The basement was full of old medical journals and cobwebs. There was no underground cavern, no secret corridors or rooms, nothing but dust and mildew."

The silence that followed was heavy with questions. Obviously the officer was beginning to suspect Mike of lying. "Okay, son, let's go back to the start and take it again."

The officer questioned Mike and Nick for another hour. Clearly he was not satisfied with their story, and when they had finished he sat tapping his pencil on the table.

"All right, Mike. Considering all the strange things that have happened to you over the last few weeks, I'm going to give you the benefit of the doubt." Then turning to Nick, "As for you, Mr. Travis, I'll be taking you with me, and calling the federal authorities. I'm sure they'll want to talk with you."

Nick nodded, then turned to Mike. "Mike, I just want to say . . . uh . . . that . . . uh . . . well, I'm sorry for everything I've done. I almost got us killed today, and, well . . . "

Sincere or not, Mike was touched by Nick's apology. "That's okay, Nick.

I just hope you'll keep it straight now."

With that, the officer and Nick left, and the group started for the Danford home.

"I'm sorry I ever doubted you, son," Mr. Danford said. "You were right about Boyd all along."

"That's okay, Dad. All I had to go on was a gut feeling."

They arrived at the house and Mrs. Danford fixed a meal for Mike, who hadn't eaten in many hours. Mike's mother and father had accepted Nick's reform, but Josh wasn't so sure.

"I just don't trust him, Mike," Josh said. He was phony about being your friend before and he could be phony now."

"Don't worry, Josh, I'm not going to trust him blindly. I *think* he's really changed, but until I'm sure I'll keep an eye on him -- assuming he even gets out of jail. If he's just tricking us, he'll slip up sooner or later. But don't forget it was because of him that I was able to escape and foul up Boyd's plan."

"Maybe that *was* Boyd's plan," Josh said.

"Maybe. But Boyd and his men were awfully good actors if it was."

"What do you think they're planning?"

"I don't know, but it's got to be big."

Mike suddenly remembered the CD he had taken from the cavern. Realizing he had left it on the sub, he got his coat and started for the door.

"Hold *it!*" Mrs. Danford's voice was stern. "Where do you think you're going?"

"I just have to run down to the sub and grab a CD I left there."

"Oh no you don't. You're staying right here where you're safe. You can listen to one of your other CD's."

"Mom, I can't stay locked inside the house the rest of my life."

"Not the rest of your life, just tonight. It's just not safe for you out there."

"What about the time you lived with the headhunters in Papua New Guinea for a month," Mike said, half-teasing his mother. "Was *that* safe?"

"That was different," Mrs. Danford said with a smile. "I was an adult, and my mother wasn't standing next to me. Besides," she said with a wink, "they were *reformed* headhunters."

Mike sighed in defeat. "I'll get it, Mike," Josh said. "No one's after me as long as I'm not with you!"

While Josh was gone, Mike explained about the CD to his parents. A few minutes later Josh returned and they put the CD in Mr. Danford's stereo. Mike turned the unit on and a series of eerie crying sounds filled the room.

"I know that sound," Josh exclaimed. "That's a pod of killer whales!"

CHAPTER FOURTEEN
A DARING PLAN

Instantly Mike knew that his friend was right. The sounds on the CD were unmistakably those of killer whales. "But why? If researching whales was just a cover, why would Boyd have thousands of dollars of equipment to edit their sounds?"

After a few seconds of quiet, Mr. Danford spoke up. "Perhaps it was just part of the cover, in case anyone ever asked to see his work. Or possibly he really *was* researching whales. After all, his main cover is being a doctor, and he actually does that as well."

They talked for a while longer, but could think of no other reason for the CD's. It was like a puzzle to Mike, though. His mind kept spinning the possibilities round and round.

As exhausted as he was, Mike still couldn't get to sleep that night. He tossed and turned, and pulled the pillow over his head. But no matter what, he couldn't stop thinking about everything that had happened, and the mysterious CD he had found.

Suddenly, it hit him like a bolt of lightening. Reaching over to Josh's bed, he shook his friend awake.

"Josh. Wake up. I've got it!"

The last thing Josh wanted to do was wake up, but Mike was insistent.

"Wake *up*! I figured out the CD!"

Josh raised his head and reluctantly opened his eyes. Without thinking, Mike turned on the lamp next to his bed.

"Aggh!" Josh dove back under the pillow.

"Sorry," Mike said, turning off the light. "Wasn't thinking."

"Okay, now that you've got my attention, what's your brilliant theory."

Mike was tingling with excitement. "Listen, all along we've assumed that the thing on the cable under BakerBoyd's boat was a hydrophone for *listening* to whale sounds." He sucked in a deep breath, almost afraid to say the next part. "What if it was really a speaker used to *make* whale noises?"

Josh thought for a moment, letting this sink in. "All right, but why? All that would do is make it easy for the Navy to track him."

"Exactly!" Mike sat up now, enthusiasm for his theory exploding inside. "The Navy would be tracking a pod of killer whales, just like they always do.

What they wouldn't realize is that those 'whales' are actually masking the sound of a moving submarine!"

Josh sat up now, too. "You mean BakerBoyd makes so much noise with the whale CD that the Navy can't hear the submarine?"

"Exactly."

The dim light filtering in from a street revealed a smile on Josh's face. "Mike, for once I think you're right!"

Mike felt his chest relax. It's been a long time since anyone believed me about *any*thing, he thought.

Josh frowned again. "But that still doesn't explain why there's a submarine here in the first place."

"Josh," Mike said intently, "what's happening at Keyport the day after tomorrow?"

Josh looked like Mike had slapped him. His mouth dropped open, and his voice cracked as he softly said, "They're launching the Nebraska!"

Mike just nodded and watched his friend follow the same string of thoughts he had.

"I'll bet they plan to torpedo it as soon as it leaves the shipyard!" Josh whispered.

Mike nodded again. "And since the Navy doesn't know the Kirovians have a submarine here, everyone will just think the explosion was caused by a flaw in the design of the Nebraska. The whole project will be tied up for years while they try to figure out what happened!"

Another thought struck Mike. "That must be who he was talking to on that microphone! I bet the Christmas tree is an underwater antenna system for talking to the Kirovian sub!"

"That's got to be it," Josh exclaimed.

"He must have used that to relay messages from Kirov to the sub, since they couldn't surface to use their radio."

"That's why BakerBoyd was in such a hurry to get out of here. I'll bet he's out there right now, telling the commander of the sub what's happened."

"And changing their plans, no doubt," Josh sighed.

Mike thought for a moment. "I don't think they'll do that. I think they'll stick with the original plan. They've obviously been planning it for months . . . maybe years. To change now would mean the loss of all that work."

"What about the Navy?" Josh asked. "BakerBoyd thinks they have his sub pinpointed."

Mike was lost in thought. "Maybe he knows they don't. When he made that first phone call back at his base, I got the impression he was talking about the submarine. He was real excited for a few minutes, then relaxed and laughed.

I think he knows the Navy doesn't believe me."

"Well, I think this is one time we need to talk to your father *before* we act."

"Agreed," Mike said.

At breakfast the next morning Mike and Josh presented their theory to Mr. Danford.

"It makes sense, Mike. It certainly seems suspicious that the Kirovians would have a submarine here just when the Navy is launching *its* newest sub."

"So what do we do?" Mrs. Danford asked.

Mike's father considered for a moment. "About all we *can* do is contact Admiral Norton and let him know our suspicions."

"Is he back from Washington D.C. yet?" It was a relief to Mike that his parents believed him at last.

"I don't know, but there's an easy way to find out. Shall I call or would you like to?"

Mike thought for a moment. "I'll do it." Going to the phone Mike quickly dialed the number for the Navy base. A moment later he spoke to someone on the other end. "Admiral Norton's office, please." Another pause. "I'd like to speak to Admiral Norton please, this is Mike Danford. Oh, I see. When will he be back? . . . Would I like to speak to Commander Ramsey?" Mike looked over at his father, who nodded. "Yes, I would, please."

Several minutes passed while Mike was on "hold". The group at the table talked quietly but Mike was becoming impatient. Josh, too, was anxious.

"I don't think they put you on hold, Mike. I think they put you on ignore."

Finally Commander Ramsey's voice came on the other end of the phone. "This is Ramsey, what can I do for you, Mike?" The commander's tone indicated he was in a hurry.

"Uh, I was just calling to give you some information, Commander."

The Navy man was obviously impatient. "Yes, what is it?"

Nervously, Mike rushed into his story. After he finished, there was silence at the other end for a few seconds. When Commander Ramsey finally spoke, Mike decided he preferred the silence.

"Look kid, I've been nice to you because you're a friend of Admiral Norton's, but this has gone far enough. I have a sub to launch in twenty-seven hours and I don't have time to play games. Yes, I heard about your so-called kidnaping. I also heard that there is absolutely no evidence to support your claim and I am not going to waste the Navy's time chasing the fantasies of some punk kid!"

Mike felt like he had been spanked in front of a school assembly. All I'm trying to do is help, he thought, and this is what I get for it!

Mr. Danford saw Mike's face turn pale then red, and guessed what was happening. Taking the phone, he spent the next several minutes trying to convince the commander, who was much more courteous to Mr. Danford than he had been to Mike.

"I know it's a wild story, Commander, but I completely believe and support my son in this matter."

"All right, Mr. Danford, what is it you want me to do?"

"That's up to you. All we have done is present you with what we believe to be a real threat to the security of this nation. It is now your responsibility to act on that information as you see fit."

There was a pause while the Navy man considered this. "You say it's your belief that this Boyd guy uses whale sounds to mask their submarine movements?"

"That is one possibility." Mr. Danford was not going to be trapped.

"Well, at this moment we are tracking a pod of whales in the middle of the sound just off Seacrest. We'll check it out. If I understand you correctly, you think we won't find any whales, but will find a cabin cruiser with Doctor Boyd on board, is that right?"

"As I said, it is one possibility."

"Fine. I'll let you know what we discover. Good day, Mr. Danford."

Mike's father relayed the conversation to the rest of his family. "Well at least he listened to you," Mike said. "He told *me* I was having fantasies!"

"I'm afraid that's a handicap of youth. Some adults will never believe that teenagers have anything valuable to offer. It's just something you have to live with, Mike."

Josh finished his third stack of pancakes and then made a suggestion. "Why don't we go down to the marina and watch the Navy through the telescope?"

The idea was instantly accepted and they all left for the marina. Mrs. Danford even left the breakfast dishes on the table, a first in the Danford home.

They climbed the weathered stairs to the observation deck on top of the marina, then took turns watching through the telescope. Eventually three small Navy ships rounded Pillar Point and entered the sound. They spread apart and began criss-crossing the water, homing in on the whale noises.

Mike scanned the water and got a sick feeling in his stomach. There were no cabin cruisers in the direction the Navy was headed. As he watched the ships converge on an area, Mike suddenly saw a spray of water erupt and a black-and-white form leap into the air.

Turning away from the telescope, Mike could barely contain his disappointment. Each of the others also looked through the spyglass, saw the pod of whales surfacing, and silently turned away.

Josh was the last to view the scene. He watched as the Navy ships circled the pod and then headed back to the base at full speed.

Mr. Danford put his arm around Mike's shoulders. "Well, this doesn't change my opinion of your theory. It's only natural for a real group of whales to be out there. After all, that's why Boyd uses that as a cover, because it's so common."

Mike was glad that his father still believed him, but couldn't help feeling frustrated. "I just keep picturing Boyd out there somewhere watching all this and laughing at us."

At home a few minutes later the phone rang and Mr. Danford answered. It was obvious to the others that the caller was Commander Ramsey, and that Mr. Danford was being scolded.

"Now just a minute, Commander, I will not accept that from you. Is it the Navy's position that citizens should not report suspicious activity to their government? Very well then, I am not sorry nor will I apologize for doing what I see as my civic duty. And you can be assured that Admiral Norton will hear of your attitude when he returns. Good day sir!"

With that, Mike's father slammed the phone down. "It is very rare that someone can make me lose my temper, but that man has a talent for it!"

The phone call had made Mike even more depressed. He and Josh were in their room talking about the situation when Mike made a decision. Sitting up on his bed his natural enthusiasm returned.

"Look. We both know what Boyd is up to. Just because Ramsey won't believe it doesn't mean it isn't true. And if the Navy won't do anything about it, then someone else will have to."

Josh looked back at his friend suspiciously. "And that someone is us?"

"That someone is us!" Mike was firm and convincing. "We have a submarine, we know how Boyd operates, and we know their plan. There's nothing to stop us from taking action!"

"Nothing except that they have a *bigger* submarine, they have *real* guns, and we don't know where *they* are." Josh always got to the heart of a problem.

"Minor details," Mike said. "We can work around those."

Resigning himself to the inevitable, Josh asked the next question. "So what's the plan. It had better be good if you expect your parents — any my mother — to go along with it."

They talked about it for more than an hour, trying to think of all the risks. Together, they worked out a plan that seemed safe and foolproof.

"Now for the tough part," Mike said. "Let's go convince my parents."

Mike's parents listened carefully as Mike explained what he wanted to do. Though they agreed the plan could work, neither of them would allow him to go through with it.

Pacing the floor, Mike tried to make them understand how he felt. "Dad, a couple hours ago you gave Commander Ramsey a lecture on civic duty and patriotism. All I'm saying is that I don't want to just talk patriotic, I want to *act* patriotic. We both know that if the Kirovians aren't stopped they'll destroy the Nebraska - a sub designed to help fight terrorists! Hundreds of men will die if it's sunk. We can stop that from happening!"

Taking a deep breath, Mike sat down and gave his final argument. "In a few months I'm going to be eighteen years old. If this country should go to war, the government can draft me and send me to some jungle somewhere to fight. As much as I don't like that idea, it might be necessary for this country to survive. When *you* were eighteen, Dad, you were in a dozen different battles in the navy. By the time she was twenty, Mom had already exposed some crooked U.N. workers in Zimbabwe. All I'm saying is that I want to do my part, but I'd rather fight here and now, of my own free will, without guns." He paused, resting his chin in his hands. "And maybe, just maybe, we can stop a war before it starts."

Mike's father looked at his wife, then back at Mike. "Son, I love you very much and I don't want to see you hurt. But you're right, and I'm very proud of you for caring so much about your country. You have my permission, and I'll help you in any way possible." He shook Mike's hand, then hugged him. "Just be careful," he whispered. "I want you around to celebrate that birthday."

With Mr. Danford's help, the boys were able to convince Josh's mother to allow Josh to be part of the plan. Then the group went to the marina to prepare the sub.

"The first thing we have to do," Mike said, "is install the remote manipulator arm I designed."

Using materials they had brought along, they began the tedious work of installing the submarine's new limb. Although they didn't know why they were doing it, Mike's boss and Jake helped with the process, which took most of the day.

Late that afternoon Josh looked up from what he was doing and saw Nick Travis approaching. "Mike!" he hissed. "Look who's coming." Mike looked over and Josh spoke what was on both their minds. "What are you going to tell him? He's sure to want to go along."

Before Mike could answer, Nick was in earshot. Smiling and obviously glad to see Mike, Nick greeted him warmly. "Hi Mike. You guys getting ready for a cruise?"

"Hi Nick. Uh, yeah, we're going to go out later tonight." Mike quickly tried to change the subject. "So how'd it go last night?"

"Okay. Jail sure isn't much fun. But this morning the federal agents came I told them everything I could about the Kirovians. They told the judge I'd been a big help, and she let me go in my uncle's custody. I can't wait to testify against Boyd when they catch him!'"

"Well, at least you're doing the right thing now." Mike was trying to think of something else to say but Nick beat him to it.

"I got to thinking about this whole thing last night, Mike, and I realized that if I were you I'd be pretty suspicious of me. After all, I fooled you once, and for all you know I might be doing it again. So I decided that, until this whole thing is over, I'm going to stay away from you and your sub, just to prove to you that I've really changed." Then lowering his voice and looking at the floor, "You're the first real friend I've ever had, Mike. I don't want to mess that up."

Mike was touched by Nick's sincerity and there was no longer any doubt in his mind. "Thank you for understanding, Nick."

The two shook hands and Nick walked away.

"Well, how about that," was Josh's only comment.

"Remind me to talk to you about something later," Mike said as he watched Nick go. Until then he had forgotten all about revealing their secret to the other boy.

Twenty minutes later the arm was finished and tested. By then it was supper time, so Mr. Danford and the boys went home to eat, and then wait. After dinner, Mike went over his plan one more time, spreading a chart on the table.

"We'll launch the sub from Seacrest, here, just after the tide change at midnight. We'll cruise to the middle of the sound and pick up the current, then shut off our motors. The Navy will hear us go to the middle of the Sound, but won't know what we're doing after that. At least not until we call them on the radio and tell them what we've done."

Moving his finger across the chart, he traced the proposed route. "We'll drift with the current north through the Tillicum Straits to the entrance of Captain's Inlet, here. If the Kirovians are going to attack the Nebraska, it will probably be there, as the sub comes out of the inlet. The water there is three thousand feet deep and it would be hard to recover any of the wreckage."

Mike stood up and stretched. "Hopefully we'll find the Kirovians before the Kirovians find the Nebraska. It shouldn't be hard if Boyd sticks to his plan."

Mr. Danford sat back and nodded. "I wish I was going with you, Mike, but you'll need to save all the oxygen you can. Besides, your mother would never allow both of us to go. Just remember that you're not to try to stop them yourselves. An unarmed mini-sub is no match for Kirovian torpedoes."

"Don't worry Dad, I'm dedicated but not stupid."

The hours until midnight dragged for the Danfords. Mike and Josh went over and over the plan, trying to find any flaws. Finally it was time to go to the marina and launch the sub. Jessica joined the group as they walked in the salty night air.

"Take a deep breath, Mike," Josh said. "It's gonna be a while before you get to smell that again!"

Standing in a circle by the sub, Mr. Danford prayed for the boys, then they gave their good wishes and goodbyes. Jessica gave Mike a goodbye kiss on the cheek, much to his embarrassment. After hugs and warnings to be careful, the two young men climbed aboard the Jonah.

The craft moved slowly down the ramp, then dropped free. With batteries and air tanks fully charged, Mike and Josh headed out to the middle of Admiralty Sound. They dove to fifty feet so the wind wouldn't blow them off course.

Mike cut the motors while Josh worked the air valves to keep them level. The current was strong and they began moving quickly. Josh sent up the buoy that held the Global Positioning System antenna, and Mike carefully tracked their progress. "Glad we have the GPS," he said, then added, "looks like we're right on course."

Once they were settled in at fifty feet, there was nothing for Mike and Josh to do but sit and wait. They had calculated it would take six hours to drift to Captain's Inlet, and they spent the time talking non-stop. Mike explained to Josh about sharing their secret with Nick, and Josh said he didn't mind at all. "I guess if God can change *my* heart, he can change Nick's too," he said.

At about five in the morning they surfaced to open the hatch, saving the bottled air for later. "We made better time than I thought we would," Mike said with a smile, "but we're on a straight line for the inlet."

The two celebrated their success so far by eating the donuts and hot chocolate Mike's mother had sent along. Knowing Josh as she did, Mrs. Danford had sent some sandwiches as well.

Just before dawn Mike announced it was time to dive again. Taking one last breath of the fresh salt air, he closed the hatch. They were approaching the mouth of the inlet, and Mike guided the sub down to the bottom, about a mile offshore.

"We should be able to hear the 'whales' easily from this position," he said. "Then all we have to do is intercept them."

The Nebraska was scheduled to be launched at eleven in the morning. It would take another half hour for it to travel to the mouth of the inlet. If Mike was right, they should be able to hear Boyd's fake whale sounds sometime before that.

They sat on the bottom, leaving the lights off to conserve the batteries. In the dim glow of the instruments Mike could see Josh listening intently to the headphones. The minutes dragged by, with Mike becoming more nervous every second. I hate waiting, he kept thinking to himself.

Just after ten Josh let out a whoop. "I've got them! Bearing two-seven-zero degrees!"

Mike wiped the sweat from his hands. He had half-expected the plan to fail, and so far it had worked perfectly. He took the headphones from Josh to listen for himself.

Off in the distance, from the direction of Admiralty Sound to the east, Mike heard the unmistakable cries of a pod of killer whales!

CHAPTER FIFTEEN
A FRIENDLY ATTACK

"Okay, this is it." Giving the phones back to Josh, Mike turned around and buckled himself in. He moved the throttles ahead slightly, then pulled back on the wheel, raising the sub off the bottom.

"At this speed they shouldn't be able to hear us," Mike said. With the propellers barely turning, he hoped no one would notice their presence until it was too late.

Josh eased an air valve forward, slowly sending a little air into the ballast tanks. At that distance, and with all the whale noises, it was doubtful that the Kirovians could have heard even a full-blown air blast, but the two were taking no chances.

"Come right about ten degrees," Josh ordered. Following the course of the whale sounds through the sonar, he estimated the point where Jonah could intercept the enemy sub.

Forty-five minutes passed as Mike and Josh slowly guided the craft in the direction of the whale noises. The temptation to go faster was strong, but Mike knew they had to take their time. As impatient as he felt, he couldn't let the Kirovians hear the Jonah.

When they were about two miles away from the whale sounds, Mike took the sub to periscope depth. Josh raised the scope and began searching the horizon.

"Hello, Mr. BakerBoyd." Josh's quiet greeting as he looked through the periscope took Mike by surprise.

"You mean he's really out there?"

"He sure is," Josh answered. "Headed right for us, slowly. Phony fishing poles and all."

Mike felt his skin tingle in excitement and he broke out in a grin. "It's going to work. It's really going to work!"

Josh pulled the periscope down and moved back to his seat. He also wore a grin, and said, "Yup, it's really going to work!" They high-fived, then went back to the serious business of finding the enemy.

At Mike's command, Josh flooded the ballast tanks, and the sub began to dive deeper under the weight.

"It's getting close," Josh announced, listening carefully on the sonar. "I'd say no more than a few hundred yards."

"Now all we have to do is find the sub in the middle of all that noise."

Cutting the throttles back, Mike hovered the Jonah a few hundred feet off the bottom, which at this point was fourteen hundred feet below the surface. "The hard part is going to be spotting the sub. It could be anywhere out here, not just in the center of the noises."

Josh already knew this, of course, but Mike was nervous and had to talk. He strained to see through the cloudy water, watching for even a hint of a shadow. He was so nervous he didn't even feel like sucking on a Jolly Rancher.

"They're almost on top of us!" Josh called. Mike could now hear the whale cries even without the sonar. A moment later another shout from Josh. "There it is!"

Looking where Josh pointed out the window, a hundred feet below them and off to the right, Mike saw the huge Kirovian sub slipping quietly by. The sight was eerie, like some giant sea monster waiting to gobble them up, and it sent a chill down Mike's spine. But since the bigger sub had no windows, and could not hear them on sonar, they had no idea the Jonah was anywhere near.

"Full flood!" Mike shouted. Instantly Josh pulled all the ballast levers, sending a torrent of water into the ballast tanks. At the same moment Mike shoved the throttles all the way forward.

Feeling like a mosquito attacking an elephant, Mike kept a steady course straight for the bridge of the monster sub. "Ready on the release arm!" he commanded. Josh gripped the lever that would open the remote control hand.

Mike saw the enemy sub start to make a sharp turn. They probably heard our motors, he thought. The big boat was too slow, however, and in seconds Mike was gliding along its top deck.

"Standby," he called to Josh. "*Now!*" At Mike's command, Josh opened the Jonah's manipulator hand. Mike had placed the sub's Emergency Locator Beacon in the hand before they left Seacrest, and it now dropped onto the Kirovian craft. A magnet on the base of the beacon attached it firmly to the enemy sub. A cable hooked to Jonah pulled a switch, and the beacon immediately began sending out a strong, low-frequency homing signal.

Moments later the sub's giant propellers spun into action, and the enemy vanished from view, out toward open water. Boyd continued his leisurely course toward the mouth of the inlet, unaware that the sub he was protecting had deserted.

Laughing and pounding each other on the back, Mike and Josh celebrated their victory. "Did you see that?" Josh asked unnecessarily. "They took off like a branded calf!"

"It was *great!*," Mike shouted. "A perfect shot. They'll be trying to shake that thing off for miles."

"But they can't," Josh said, laughing. "They'd have to surface to get it off, and then the Navy would get them!"

Wiping tears of joy from his eyes, Mike turned back to steering the Jonah. In all his life he had never had such a feeling of relief.

"We'd better get up there and tell the Navy what's going on," Mike said, still with a smile. A picture of the emergency beacon dropping neatly onto the enemy sub kept replaying in his mind.

Putting the Jonah at full speed again, Mike brought it up to five hundred feet and headed for the inlet. "We'll have to get around the end of the peninsula so our radio signals can get through," he said.

Josh was still listening to the sonar. "The Kirovians are heading out to sea. That ole beeper is still going strong!" A moment later his glee turned to curiosity. "Hey, I've picked up another set of propellers overhead. Sounds like they're coming this way."

"It must be a Navy ship," Mike concluded. "Let's go up and check it out."

Before they had reached three hundred feet, Josh made another comment. "That's strange. I just heard a big splash and then a clicking sound."

Mike spun around and exchanged horrified looks with Josh as they both realized what the sound meant. Before either could say anything, a series of explosions rocked the boat.

Wham! Wham! Wham! The concussion from the depth charges smashed into the sub with such force that Mike couldn't believe it didn't split open.

"They're coming back!" Josh yelled, imagining more of the large barrels of explosives being dropped off the back of the Navy ship.

Terror gripped Mike's throat like a razor-sharp claw. "We've got to surface," he squeaked. "We've got to let them know it's us!"

But before they could do anything another series of charges went off, this time closer.

Wham Wham Wham Wham! It was like some huge sledge hammer smashing the hollow steel boat. Each new hit pounded Mike's eardrums until he could no longer hear.

Josh pulled the levers that sent air into the tanks, while Mike pulled back hard on the wheel. He looked up from the instrument panel and let out a yell. Fifteen feet in front of him he saw three more ugly depth charges floating downward. If they go off this close, he thought, we're dead.

The drums drifted past and time seemed to stop. Mike sat waiting for the explosion he knew was coming. His hands were slippery with sweat, and his whole body was drenched. Holding on to his seat, he began praying out loud, and heard Josh do the same.

WHAM WHAM WHAM! The violent eruption of the charges lifted the tiny sub and then slammed it down again. Water sprayed down on Mike as the front bubble sprang a leak where it joined the hull. The craft spun wildly as if it were in some giant washing machine, and he no longer knew which way was up.

"Please *God, help us*!" Josh's screamed prayer came from somewhere behind Mike. He tried to concentrate on getting control of the sub, but depth charges kept going off in his mind. Without warning another series of real bombs exploded.

WHAM WHAM WHAM WHAM WHAM! These were the closest yet, and three more seams broke loose. Water was pouring into the sub now and Mike knew they had only seconds to react. Reaching behind him, he pulled the lever that sent compressed air inside the sub. Used to test the sub's water tightness, Mike hoped this action would slow the incoming torrent of water.

The flood of water slowed to a stream as the air pressure held the water at bay. Needles of pressure poked at his eardrums, but Mike knew this was better than drowning. Once again he pulled back on the wheel and headed for what he thought was the surface. The attacking ship was so close now that he could hear its screaming engines even without the sonar.

The high-pitched whine of the approaching propellers drowned out all other sound. This is our last chance, Mike thought. He watched the depth gauge, and held the throttles full open. Gaining speed the closer they got to the surface, the Jonah shot through the water like a torpedo.

Only fifty feet to go, but the cruiser overhead was already launching her depth charges. But then brilliant sunlight punched Mike in the face as the Jonah broke through the surface and shot into the air. The hull came slamming down on the water again with a shudder.

Mike scrambled for the radio microphone. Before he had a chance to speak, a tower of water erupted around them as the final depth charges exploded far below. With the water still raining down on them, Mike pushed the button and yelled into the microphone.

"This is the Jonah, the Jonah . . . the United States Ship *Jonah*. Don't shoot! We're a private submarine. We are unarmed. *Stop shooting*!"

A moment of static was broken by a familiar voice. "This is Admiral Norton to all Navy vessels. *Cease fire*! Repeat, *do not* fire." Then a moment later, "Admiral Norton to Jonah . . . is that you, Mike?"

"Yes sir! We followed a Kirovian sub out here. We were just coming to contact you when your ships started attacking us."

"I don't know what's going on down there, Mike," the admiral said. "I'm just now arriving back from Washington D.C. But I guarantee that you're safe now. Are you all right? Do you need any help?"

Mike looked around. The sub had stopped leaking, and there was only a few inches of water in the bilge. "We're okay now, sir."

"I'm in a helicopter headed your way, Mike. Can you meet me over at that cruiser on your right?"

"Gladly!"

Within minutes the Jonah was tied up alongside the ship that moments before had tried to sink her. Admiral Norton's helicopter landed, and soon he was asking a lot of questions.

Mike told the whole story of his kidnaping, and about Commander Ramsey's reaction when Mike told him about it. At that point the captain of the cruiser broke in.

"Commander Ramsey is the one who ordered me to depth-charge the small sub. We had picked up propeller noise from two submarines, a big one and a small one. Commander Ramsey told us to ignore the big sub and go after the little one. I tried to convince him otherwise, but he ordered me to do it."

Admiral Norton's fury spread across his face. "And what of the other sub? Is anyone chasing it?"

"No sir, not that I know of."

Turning back to Mike, the admiral asked one more question. "You say that you planted a marker buoy on the sub?"

"Yes sir," Mike answered. "It's transmitting on forty-three point five kilohertz."

The admiral swiftly gave orders for several ships to chase down the enemy sub. He also ordered the capture of Doctor Boyd's cabin cruiser, and a better search of Boyd's house.

"Mike, Josh, we not only owe you an apology, but a wealth of gratitude as well," the admiral said. "You have undoubtedly saved the Nebraska from certain destruction." Looking across the bow of the cruiser, he pointed toward the inlet. "In fact, there she is now."

Mike watched with pride as the sleek outline of America's latest submarine sliced through the water of Admiralty Sound. He had to grab the railing to hold steady as all the joy and fear and excitement and frustration he'd felt over the last months drained from his body. With a tear in his eye, he realized that he and Josh had saved the hundreds of lives on board the Nebraska.

You never know what God has planned!" The old man's words from weeks before came crashing in from Mike's memory. Remembering that early morning walk on the beach, and how he'd almost given up, Mike slowly shook his head. "No, you never do know," he whispered.

And then he popped a Jolly Rancher in his mouth.

A week later Mike, Josh, and their families were guests at the Keyport Naval Base. A banquet was held in honor of the two young men, with reporters and television cameras almost outnumbering the Navy personnel. Jordan, Captain Washington, Jake and Jessica had a front row table.

In a speech that lasted twenty minutes, Admiral Norton detailed the events that led up to the banquet.

"So to summarize," he said, "a dangerous terrorist group has been arrested, a Kirovian submarine has been confiscated, a secret underground base has been uncovered, and the United States Ship Nebraska has been saved from destruction. All because of the brave and patriotic acts of these two young men."

The admiral motioned for Mike and Josh to stand. "And so it is with honor and gratitude, and on behalf of the President of the United States, that I present Michael James Danford and Joshua Allen Roberts with the highest award bestowed on civilians, the Department of Defense Distinguished Public Service Award, for their exceptional devotion to duty and extremely significant contributions to the defense of our country."

The audience exploded with a standing ovation as the admiral hung large gold medals around the necks of the boys. And Mike noticed with pleasure that the applause was led by Nick Travis in the front row. After making acceptance speeches and answering reporters' questions, Mike, Josh, and their families were ushered into the Admiral's office.

"I couldn't mention this out there," the admiral said, indicating the banquet room, "but there was one other development as a result of this. Commander Ramsey has been arrested as a member of the Revolutionary Army of Kirov."

Mrs. Danford gasped, and Mike stared at the admiral in shock. "How did he get to be a Commander?" Mike asked.

"He and his parents were planted here years ago as spies. He grew up and joined the Navy like any young American might, and worked his way up through the ranks. All that time he was able to keep his real identity a secret. Thanks to Mike and Josh, he had to blow his cover and we found him out."

Mike's father nodded.

Admiral Norton continued. "As you suspected, Mike, Doctor Boyd was the local contact for the Kirovian sub. The strange device on the bottom of his boat was an antenna which transmitted on a very low frequency. Its special design allowed Boyd to talk to the sub directly below him, without being picked up by any other radio. You were right about the sphere, as well. Whenever the sub had to move, Boyd would lower the speaker a few hundred feet and start playing the whale sounds. The sub could then move without us hearing it."

Mike started to ask a question, but Josh asked it first. "Why didn't Boyd change his plans after Mike told him we had pictures of the sub?"

"He started to. Boyd tried to contact Ramsey, but Ramsey was off the base at the time, so Boyd decided to abandon the plan. That's when you saw him packing, Mike. He had no way of knowing that I was in Washington D.C. and couldn't possibly have talked to you."

"By the time Boyd found this out," the admiral continued, "Mike and Nick had already escaped. After that, Ramsey assured Boyd that the Navy didn't believe Mike. Of course, this was true, since the *real* Navy hadn't even heard Mike's story."

"Why didn't the police find anything when they searched Boyd's house?" Mike asked. "And why did they build the complex in the first place?"

"The underground cavern could only be reached by a secret elevator which was well hidden in the basement. It took a crack team of specialists from the FBI several hours to find it, so it's no wonder the local police missed it. The Kirovians were building the complex to house mini-subs of their own. Once operational, they could have transferred equipment and terrorists from the big sub to the mainland at any time without being detected."

After a moment of silence, Mike's father spoke up. "If you're finished, Admiral, I have a surprise of my own for Mike." The admiral nodded and Mr. Danford continued. "I was contacted by a boat-building firm this week. They would like to buy the patent for your sub, Mike. They saw it on one of Mr. Stevenson's advertisements, and have offered a considerable sum of money. Plus a royalty on every submarine they sell."

For once Mike couldn't think of anything to say. "I . . . I . . . I . . . ."

The group laughed, and Josh pounded his friend on the back. "Just think, Mike, with all that money you can buy me dinner every night!"

"Oh no," Mike groaned. "One minute I'm rich, the next I'm broke!" Then reconsidering, "No, as long as I have friends and family like you, and a God who loves me, I'll be the richest man in the world."

And so he was.

Now that you're done reading the book . . .

Ask Mom or Dad if you can go to our website. There you'll find:
- loads of other information about Mike, Josh, and the others
- Mike's sketches of the submarine
- a quiz to test your knowledge of the story
- Bible verses that go with the story
- maps of Seacrest and Admiralty Sound
- and much more!

www.JerichoQuill .com

Other books by Arnold Ytreeide

Check out our website for these and other titles:

The Jotham's Journey Trilogy – adventure books for the whole family to be read during the Christmas season or any other time:

- **Jotham's Journey**
- **Bartholomew's Passage**
- **Tabitha's Travels**

During Lent and the Easter season, or whenever you want another adventure:

- **Mystery of the Temple Court**

Just for fun!

- **Under My Teacher's Desk**

Visit our website for more books for **kids, teens, and adults!**

www.JerichoQuill.com

2170255

Made in the USA